DAVID JONES

BABOON

A NOVEL

annick press
toronto + new york + vancouver

Text © 2007 David Jones
Second printing, October 2007

Annick Press Ltd.

We acknowledge the support of the Canada Council for the Arts, the Ontario Arts Council, the Government of Canada through the Book Publishing Industry Development Program (BPIDP), and the Ontario Book Publishing Tax Credit (OBPTC) for our publishing activities.

Edited by Pam Robertson
Copy edited and proofread by Melissa Edwards
Cover and interior design by Irvin Cheung + Chris Freeman / iCheung Design, inc.
Cover model, Kieran McCord
Interior illustrations by Chris Freeman

Cover photos: (baboon) © Michael K. Nichols/National Geographic/Getty Images; (boy) © Irvin Cheung

Special thanks to Dr. Robert Sapolsky, Stanford University, research associate with the Institute of Primate Research at the National Museum of Kenya, for his expertise in reviewing the manuscript.

Cataloguing in Publication

Jones, David (David Richard), 1956-
    Baboon : a novel / by David Jones.

ISBN-13: 978-1-55451-054-2 (bound)
ISBN-10: 1-55451-054-6 (bound)
ISBN-13: 978-1-55451-053-5 (pbk.)
ISBN-10: 1-55451-053-8 (pbk.)

    1. Baboons—Juvenile fiction. I. Title.

PS8619.O5323B32 2007   jC813'.6   C2006-906019-3

Published in the U.S.A. by	**Distributed in Canada by**	**Distributed in the U.S.A. by**
Annick Press (U.S.) Ltd.	Firefly Books Ltd.	Firefly Books (U.S.) Inc.
	66 Leek Crescent	P.O. Box 1338
	Richmond Hill, ON	Ellicott Station
	L4B 1H1	Buffalo, NY 14205

Printed and bound in Canada

Visit our website at **www.annickpress.com**

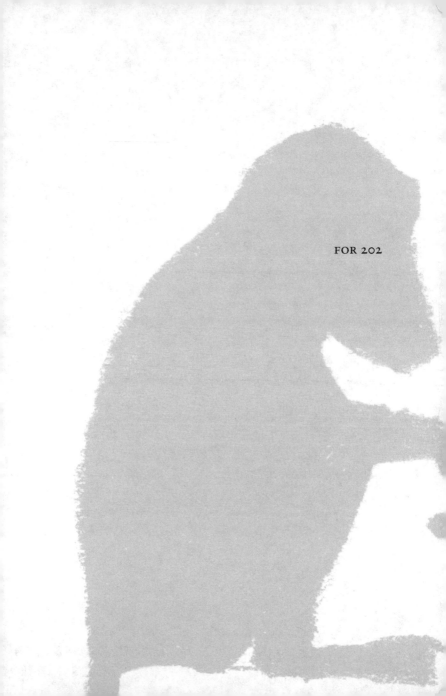

FOR 202

DESCENT

He watched a drop of water crawl up the window and dribble away, carried on the plane's slipstream. Gerry pressed his cheek to the plastic, trying to see what lay in their flight path. Ahead, anvils of cloud massed on the horizon. Lightning stabbed earthward from one of them and Gerry counted off the seconds to the thunderclap. One, one thousand...two, one thousand...three, one thousand...and then a drumroll of thunder. Only four miles now. They were still heading into the storm.

He looked across the aisle and saw his parents at their windows. Their attention was fixed on the grassland rolling below them. The pilot banked into a turn to give them a better view and Gerry caught himself gripping the arms of his seat.

"We're not going to see anything in this weather," said his mother. "I'm sure they've all taken shelter." She was talking about the troop, of course: the baboons his parents had been studying for close to three years now. The plane rolled back into level flight.

Gerry and his parents were flying back to their camp after a trip to Arusha to pick up supplies and check their e-mail. Even during that short trip, Gerry had heard his mother say more than once that she missed the troop. She wondered aloud how Zeus was doing. Was Mavis's daughter all right? Was Oscar still nursing? Had Hector's tail healed? His father would put an arm around her and try to reassure her. "They'll be fine," he said. "They managed before we ever began watching them and they'll manage long after we've stopped."

But Gerry sometimes thought his mother believed that only her constant fretting kept the troop well. His father was quieter about it, but neither of them could wait to return to camp where making field notes on baboon behavior would be their sole occupation—that and Gerry's schooling, a task they shared during the months they all lived in the field.

To tell the truth, he was relieved to be out of school for half the year. He didn't mind the classes, but in the hallways and on the playing field he had to face the fact that he was something of a runt. Just keeping up during the lunch-hour soccer games was getting harder and harder as the players around him metamorphosed into giants. "You'll shoot up," his father told him. Easy for him to say. Gerry had seen pictures of his father as a child. He guessed he had been the only elementary school student with a five o'clock shadow. No wonder he felt a special kinship with the hairier primates.

His mother crossed the aisle and kneeled in the seat in front of Gerry. She draped her elbows over the seatback and studied him.

"You all right?" she asked.

"Yep."

"Going to miss the big city?"

"The big city of Arusha? Or London?"

"I hadn't even thought of Arusha. We were only there two days. You missing that, too?"

"I already kind of miss plumbing. And television. The Internet. Restaurants—"

"Oh, and there's something wrong with *my* cooking?"

"No. But it's not like I can just order whatever I want."

"You've got that right."

"Anyway, I don't know why you're asking. It's not like if I say 'yes' we're going to turn around and go home."

"You know, there'll come a time when you look back on these days—"

"I know: the best three years of my life."

His mother sighed. "You've got us all figured out, haven't you?"

What's to figure out? he thought. *The most important thing in the world to you is a bunch of monkeys. There's nothing wrong with that. Really. There are worse things someone could devote their life to. But did you ever think I might not feel the same way?*

She returned to her seat on the other side of the cabin. A bright flash and a crack of thunder brought Gerry back to the task at hand, which was keeping the Shorts Skyvan flying. He didn't think of himself as a nervous flyer; it was just something that had to be done. Their pilot, Stan, seemed entirely too relaxed a man for the job and his parents had the troop to worry about. That left only Gerry to keep the groaning forty-year-old boxcar in the air. Clutching it by the armrests and pulling upward seemed to be working nicely, but who knew how long that was going to last?

There were only three rows of three seats, just behind the cockpit. On his parents' side of the cabin were two seats per row, on Gerry's, only one. Stan had salvaged them from a commercial airliner and bolted them to the deck of the Skyvan. They looked strangely out of place here, with their fold-down trays and headphone sockets.

He was grateful that he and his parents were the only passengers aboard. Even so, they felt heavier than they had on the flight out. *Probably all that rich restaurant food in Arusha.* That, and a small front-end loader called a Bobcat, about a ton of drilling machinery, and a stack of core boxes all filling the rear of the plane's boxy interior. Gerry guessed that the equipment was on its way to a mining camp somewhere.

He wished they were back in the city. Even another night in Arusha would be welcome. In the lineup to see a movie, a girl had waited ahead of him. He had stood right behind her, only inches away, pretending his parents were strangers. He would have said something to her if they hadn't been there. That, and if he had the slightest idea of how to start a conversation with a girl. "Hello. I couldn't help but notice that you speak English. I, too, speak English…"

Crickets chirping.

"...whenever I can think of something to say."

But all he could think of was how easy it was for males in the troop: picking your way through the grass, looking for roots, you work your way toward her. At the right moment, casually start grooming the back of her head. No need for small talk. The only reason to open your mouth is to pop in anything you find crawling through her fur. Hair.

"You're losing it, Gerry," was what his friend Milton would have said. "Out there in the jungle. It's only a matter of time."

"It's not the jungle," said Gerry. "It's the veldt."

"The what?"

"The veldt. Savanna. Grassland. It's sort of like a lawn nobody's mowed for a million years."

"Whatever. It's still the middle of nowhere. Living in a tent is not normal. You're growing up weird."

Milton's e-mails were full of such dire pronouncements—if not about their own futures, then the world at large. Global warming. Overfishing. Industrial growth in China. Rogue asteroids. Gerry's father referred to Milton as the world's grimmest thirteen-year-old. It was hard to imagine a place safer than Croydon, a comfortable suburb of London. But for Milton it was a cliff, and they were all teetering on the edge. He was right about one thing, though: living in a tent for months on end with only his parents and a troop of baboons for company wasn't exactly normal. But then, how normal was living in Croydon for the other half of the year and walking to school each morning with the prophet of doom?

Gerry missed those walks, and he liked to think that Milton missed them, too. Milton might have been glum, but they always ended up laughing about it—okay, Gerry always ended up laughing about it. Exchanging e-mails in a library or an Internet café every six weeks was no substitute for having a friend who was just two doors down the street, always there, ready to remind you that no matter how bad things might be now, in the end, they would be even worse.

The plane bucked beneath them and all three passengers grabbed their seats before they settled again into level flight. *Mind on the plane,* thought Gerry.

"Sorry, folks," said the pilot. "It's getting a little lumpy up here."

Gerry checked out the window and saw what must be the Loseya snaking beneath them, its water black beneath the leaden sky. Nearly home.

There was another flash of lightning accompanied by a BANG that shook the aircraft. Gerry knew immediately that it wasn't thunder—the sound came right on top of the flash. His father turned toward the cockpit and rose halfway out of his seat, looking through the open door.

And then a chill passed through Gerry, despite the clammy heat of the plane's cabin. Something was streaming over the engine cowling in dirty, brown fingers. It was as if the Skyvan had punctured one of those thunderheads he had seen on the horizon. It took a second for Gerry to realize what it was. Oil.

The plane's starboard engine and wing were awash in a brown sludge. "What is it?" his father shouted. He was moving up the aisle toward the cockpit.

Gerry's mother was frozen in her seat, staring out the window. She looked over and noticed Gerry. "It's all right," she said automatically. "We'll be all right."

And then Gerry saw the propeller spin to a stop, and at the same time felt a sickening loss of balance as the plane sank beneath them.

"We've blown a seal!" shouted the pilot. "And we're too heavy to hold this altitude with only one engine!"

Gerry's mother crossed the aisle and sat on the armrest of Gerry's seat.

"It's all right," she repeated.

"Mayday. Mayday. This is tango alpha echo three three niner, 105 miles out of Arusha heading one eight zero. We have lost right engine and are losing altitude. Mayday. Mayday." Then, to Gerry's father, "Ian, see if you can lighten our load!"

"What?"

"Throw out anything that isn't nailed down. Start with that Bobcat!"

His father edged past the front-end loader toward the back of the bucking plane.

"The switch for the door is just above the—"

"I see it!" shouted his father. He flipped the switch and a ramp dropped slowly from the ceiling, opening the whole back end of the plane. Dust and paper swirled around and the cabin filled with the roar of the one working engine.

"Gerry. Help me!"

Gerry undid his seatbelt and rose on wobbly legs. He staggered to the rear of the plane and leaned into the Bobcat's roll cage.

"On three!" shouted his father. Ian reached into the machine's tiny cabin and pushed the shift lever into neutral. "One...two...*three!*" They pushed, but nothing happened. Then Gerry's father found a strap lashing the machine to the deck and undid it. They pushed again and now the Bobcat rolled down the cabin.

"Okay, stay back!" yelled his father, trundling it to the head of the open ramp.

Gerry watched the machine pitch over the edge and disappear. He ran to the opening and looked down. In a flash of lightning, he caught a glimpse of the machine—a toy tumbling earthward.

"Keep going!" shouted Stan. "Anything!"

Gerry and his mother dragged a box of drill core back to Ian. He pushed it out over the lip of the opening. Gone.

It took all three of them to drag the motor for a rock drill to the edge of the ramp and roll it off.

Another box of drill core.

"It's no use!" shouted Stan. "I'm going to have to put her down. Better strap in!"

Gerry's father turned from the cockpit. "You heard him. Seatbelts!"

"I'm staying with Gerry," said his mother.

"All right, but hurry. Get your seatbelts on!"

Gerry and his mother took two of the tandem seats on the left side of the plane. Ian took the single seat across the aisle from them. They all buckled in and then Joan took their hands—his and then her husband's across the aisle. Gerry was surprised by the strength of her grip, and he returned it.

"Stan is a good pilot. We'll be all right," said his father. But on his face was a look Gerry had never seen before, and there were many times he had seen Ian Copeland with reason to be frightened. Once, while photographing an elephant with her calf, he had strayed too close. He had never seen his father run before, not like that, and as he raced toward the car Gerry was amazed at his speed. But even then the look on his face was more determination than fear. He had simply done what he had to.

But now there was nothing to do, only wait for the ground to meet them. They had already been flying low in hopes of spotting the troop and so they had very little altitude to lose.

And then the other engine stopped. From the cockpit, Gerry heard Stan cursing—every swear word Gerry had ever heard in his life, and some he hadn't.

A road swept by below them, two muddy ruts in the grass. Then they passed over the green canopy of a grove of umbrella trees.

They glided along with only the sound of their thudding hearts, the oily slapping of the wiper blades and the clicking of switches from the cockpit as Stan shut down the plane's electrical system, still cursing his mechanic, the government, the plane, lightning, Africa, the ground. All to blame. All funneling him to this landing. *God, please let it be a landing!*

The sea of grass rolled beneath the plane. It was hard to tell how high they were in the flat light, but then a flash of lightning branded the cross of their shadow on the rushing veldt. Soon now!

Their wing clipped the branch of an enormous lone olive tree, and Gerry had a glimpse of a vervet monkey scrambling inside the opened wound.

They hit hard. The impact dealt a sledgehammer blow to the bottom of his seat and they were airborne again. For one relieved moment Gerry thought they would be all right: the first impact would have to be the worst. But the plane began to cartwheel and he felt himself pitch forward against the strap of his seatbelt. They hit again, this time much harder. He saw the whole box of the fuselage buckle between himself and his father's seat, pinching the plane in half as the tail folded upwards and the broken end gouged grass and earth from the ground and sprayed it into his face. A moment of darkness, and then the cabin ripped open. As if on some terrible ferris wheel, he saw clouds wheeling and his mother, still in her seat, torn from his grasp and flung skyward before an acacia tree came tearing through the cabin, its branches clawing at everything in a racket of splintering wood. He felt a cold splash across his face and the smell of gasoline filled his nostrils.

Then came a blinding pain in the side of his head and it was dark.

GERRY AWOKE TO A DROP OF WATER hitting his eye and seeping under the half-open lid. He finished opening that eye, and then the other. He was lying on his back, looking up into the rain. The drops fell on his face and into his open mouth. It was dark now, but light shivered inside a cloud and lit up the grass around him, and then thunder pealed across the veldt.

He couldn't move. Not his head nor his hands nor his legs. All he could do was blink.

He listened and couldn't even hear his breath, just the soft plinking of the rain.

Out of the dark, he saw some baboons come out from the horizon of his vision. It was as if he could see them gathering from a great distance. Tiny at first, they came toward him through the grass and the rain and the night. They seemed to travel with a purpose, growing larger as they came. When they arrived at his side, Gerry saw that they weren't really baboons—at least they were like none he had ever seen.

Maybe it was because of how they towered over him, with nothing to compare them to but the ragged clouds tearing across the night sky, but they seemed enormous. They were more like monuments to baboons, and, in a flash of lightning, he saw that they had no eyes.

That wasn't right. They had eyes, but the eyes had no centers—no pupils or irises—making them look even more like ancient statues. Yet, from the tilt of their muzzles, dripping with rain, he knew that they were looking down at him. They lifted their heads and looked from one to another and something seemed to pass between those featureless eyes.

There was a gap in the circle of their silent council. They all turned to the opening and again, as if it was approaching from some great distance, he watched a last baboon come over the rim of his vision and close the circle.

This one was different. It really did have no eyes. Where they should have been there were only dark holes—like the eyes of a mask, waiting to be put on.

This last baboon bent over him and leaned closer with its empty eyes until its face was all that Gerry could see. Its muzzle was nearly touching Gerry's nose. He thought, if this were real, I should feel its breath on my face; I should smell it. But then he thought it had to be real, because he could no longer feel the rain. The face hanging over him was shielding him from the storm.

He felt the tip of its muzzle touch his nose, and then something even stranger happened: the face—how could he put it?—the face *everted*. From the tip of the muzzle backward, like a glove pulled from a hand, it turned inside out and seemed to envelop Gerry until now he peered out through the eyes of the mask.

What he saw was the baboon circle, all save one, looming over him. They looked from one to the other with their sightless eyes. And, one by one, they turned away and passed from the edges of his view, leaving only the clouds above him and the rain tapping at his face.

THE VELDT

The next time Gerry opened his eyes, he was lying on his side, looking at a group of quite ordinary baboons. There were at least five of them, one very close. He could have reached out and touched it—not that he would have advised doing such a thing. He was sure the baboon was Hector, one of about forty in the troop his parents studied. He had never been this close to him, but he recognized the kink in his tail.

Like the others, Hector was digging for something with his deft, black hands. Gerry watched him insert a forefinger into the soil and cut around a shoot with a quick sawing motion. Hooking his finger, he pulled a corm from the ground. He wiped it on his arm to brush off the loose dirt, examined it, and then bit into the root. Three more bites and the corm was gone. The monkey started probing for the next one. He glanced once at Gerry, then looked away, which struck Gerry as odd.

It was then he noticed something wrong with his vision. The color of everything seemed subtly altered, like a photograph left out in the sun. He blinked deliberately, as if by doing so he might clear it up. But it wasn't a problem of clarity. In fact, things were remarkably clear. The storm had scrubbed the air of dust and now the earth was beginning to steam under the late-afternoon sun.

Then Gerry remembered the storm and the crash. As he tried to get up he saw that he was lying on a thin, hairy arm ending in a hand. It was a baboon's hand. He must have been thrown clear of the wreckage and landed on one of the poor animals. Startled, he pushed himself to a sitting position and looked around.

Now the baboons reacted. Spooked by his sudden movement, they all stopped what they were doing and stared at him. Gerry froze. As his head cleared, he realized the seriousness of his situation. He was amazed that they hadn't run away or threatened him. Apart from their natural instincts to flee from people, if they had seen him fall on a baboon, they must have realized that he was dangerous—if only out of clumsiness.

And then they all returned to foraging, as if there were nothing out of the ordinary about a boy falling out of the sky and crushing one of them. But when Gerry looked to where he had been lying a moment ago, he saw nothing but a patch of flattened grass.

Without thinking, he reached up to shade his eyes and saw that same thin baboon's hand coming at his face. He flinched, and the hand stopped. For a long moment he just stared at the creased, black palm and the five delicate fingers.

He wiggled his fingers.

The fingers wiggled.

It was his own arm he was seeing.

To prove it, he turned the hand slowly from back to front before his eyes. He felt a soft grunt that started in his chest and rose in his throat. He looked down and saw his body.

Somehow, he was a baboon. Or rather, his mind was residing in a baboon's body.

Wait. Wait. That couldn't be. There was something he was missing, some...

He brought a hand to his face. He had been about to press it to his forehead and comb his fingers back through his hair, as he usually did when he was upset, only there was no forehead. His hand—that thin, black baboon's hand—was one moment at eye level and the next touching a bristled brow of hair, and then above that...air.

He had no forehead.

For some reason, that was much more frightening to him than having a baboon's hands. He paced in circles, trying to get away from this ridiculous idea that was, moment by moment, becoming more real. By now the other baboons—Ha! Other baboons—were staring at him and beginning to move away from this freak running in circles and wiping the air over his head.

Nope. Still nothing there. Still no forehead. Still a baboon.

He had to be dreaming. Or worse, he must have suffered some kind of brain damage in the crash.

Again, he remembered the plane crash.

Where were his parents? What if they needed his help? But this was followed immediately by an even more ridiculous thought: *they mustn't find out*. His father, especially, would be very unhappy with him if he were a baboon. *What are you doing in there, Gerry? These are very serious animals. They're not toys.*

As he looked around, he decided that he was having some sort of hallucination. He must have survived the crash and received medical attention. Perhaps he had been anaesthetized, and this was his reaction to the drug: some kind of vivid dreaming. He stood up as far as he could on his haunches and looked beyond the foraging troop. One of the other baboons watched Gerry, then followed his gaze around the savanna.

They were nearing the end of the rainy season, and the grass, tall and green, looped its way to the hills in the distance. Here and there were groves of acacia trees.

The next thing that Gerry noticed was the clarity of his far vision. He could pick out leaves on trees and blades of grass halfway to the horizon. He *must* be having some kind of dream—it was too real to be real. He didn't feel any pain, either.

And you couldn't live through a crash that tears a plane in two and not feel some kind of pain if you were conscious. Not a bruise or a broken bone. Surely he was drugged and dreaming.

He was right next to a big acacia tree, and Gerry decided to try walking around it. He kept trying to stand up but soon realized that he was at his full height, at least as long as he kept all four paws on the ground. He felt like he was crawling, not walking. He circled the tree slowly, so as not to call too much attention to himself. It took him a few circuits to get the hang of the baboon's gliding stride. Left front, right rear followed by right front, left rear. Left, right, left, right. That seemed to work. He stopped and watched Hector take a few paces. Yeah, that was it. He wondered how long he would have to think about walking. Four legs. It was a lot to keep track of.

The third time he rounded the tree he saw the wreckage of the plane, about 100 yards away. He just stood there, staring at it. Then, as if to confirm what he was seeing, he raised his arm so that he could take a look at his hand again.

Still a baboon.

This was really weird. What if he were all right in every way except that he somehow perceived himself to be a baboon? He'd heard of people with brain damage having some very strange reactions to their injuries.

What if his mother and father were lying in the wreckage, in far worse shape than he was? Injured? Or worse?

What if they were dead?

He didn't want to go. But he had to go. What if they needed him? He knew they wouldn't have hesitated a second. They would be looking for him, panicked.

Without thinking, he broke into a kind of gallop. He was surprised at the ease with which he covered the distance. He wasn't even breathing hard as he slowed to a walk again, now only a stone's throw from the wreck.

The plane had ended up in two pieces. He thought he remembered the cabin tearing in two, just behind the cockpit, right in front of his seat. But somehow the floor had only bent and now the whole thing had closed up again so that the cabin seemed more or less intact. One of the wings had snapped off—probably while the plane was cartwheeling after their first impact. The blades of both propellers were bent. Pieces of undercarriage were strewn over the grass. The stench of gasoline was overpowering, but Gerry was relieved. Through some miracle, there had been no fire. He remembered seeing his mother flung from the cartwheeling plane. At the front of the plane he saw a bloody crater of cracks in the cockpit window, where someone inside had struck it.

Then he saw a man climb from the cabin door. It was his father. One leg of his pants was streaked in blood and he walked with a limp but he looked amazingly well considering the wreckage he had just left. Gerry took two steps toward him and stopped. He tried to call him, but all that came out was something between a bark and a cough. His father turned, saw him, then looked away. He was searching for something.

"Gerry…! Joan…?" He kept calling their names.

Then his father was limping away from him over the grass, toward a pair of seats lying on their side. Gerry saw that his mother was strapped into one of them. His father knelt beside her and Gerry was relieved to hear his mother's voice—quite clear despite the distance. "Where's Gerry?" she was saying. "Is he all right?"

His father was undoing her seatbelt when the truck came. It left the road and bounced over the grass toward them—an ancient, creaking van with the word EMERGENCY painted on the side. Two paramedics in clean but threadbare uniforms got out.

Gerry tried to think where they would have come from. There was an airport at Kondoa, but that was hours away by road. They must have heard Stan's Mayday call and sent out a search plane, which had probably dropped the paramedics at the nearest airstrip. Maybe Ndedo.

One of the medics went straight to his mother while the other retrieved a case from the back of the van. That was when Gerry saw his own body. It was a short distance away but he recognized his shirt. He was lying on his back and one leg was twisted at an odd angle. It was obviously broken and it hurt Gerry just to look at it. He forced himself to approach it, afraid of what he would see. He started walking toward the body. *His* body.

It was not until he saw his own face that Gerry realized he wasn't just out of his mind, he was out of his body. It was impossible, but here it was: the vessel that had carried him for the last fourteen years lay sprawled in the grass. It wasn't a picture or a bad dream. It was real.

There was only one conclusion: he was dead, and the myths of reincarnation were real. Of all the beliefs about what happens to you once you die—of ghosts and heaven and hell—this must be the truth. And, if it were true, then every person who had ever died had stood like this, looking at his own body through the eyes of some animal.

He was afraid. He felt himself trembling, felt all the strength drain from his limbs and puddle beneath him.

His father was pulling one of the paramedics by the arm toward Gerry. "Help my son," he said.

The paramedic and his father knelt by the body. The medic

checked Gerry's pulse and put the mirror of his stethoscope near his mouth.

"He's alive." The paramedic removed a hypodermic syringe from his kit and began unwrapping it. Gerry's father stood up. He looked directly at Gerry—Gerry as he was now—sitting no more than twenty feet away.

It's me, Gerry wanted to shout. *I'm here, Dad!* He took a step toward him.

Gerry could hardly believe what he saw next. His father stooped, picked up a rock the size of an orange, and threw it. Gerry had to dodge it to keep from being hit. *It's me, Dad!* he tried to shout, but all that came out was something between a grunt and a bark.

"Scat!" his father shouted. "Go on!"

No, no. I'm your son! I'm here!

His father picked up another rock and winged it at Gerry. "Go on, get out of here!"

Gerry dodged the rock and retreated a few steps. He had never before felt so helpless. There must be some way to show his father who he was. If only he would let him come closer!

The paramedic glanced up and frowned. "That's a bold one," he said as he worked.

"How is he?" asked his father, returning his attention to Gerry's body.

"His vital signs are very odd."

"What do you mean, odd?"

The paramedic shook his head. "I mean his heartbeat is strong and regular but it's...so slow." He pointed to the ambulance. "There's an oxygen cylinder in the back."

His father went to the ambulance and returned with the tank.

"Are you the pilot?" The paramedic took a clear plastic mask attached to the cylinder by a hose and strapped it onto Gerry's face. He opened a valve.

"The pilot's dead," he heard his father say.

"Are you absolutely sure?"

"Yes."

His father looked up and stared again at Gerry. He found another stone. It wasn't large, but this one hit Gerry in the ribs and it hurt. A surge of rage swept over him and he charged the men, howling. He heard a series of sharp, threatening grunts and realized that the sound was coming from his own throat. He stopped just short of his human body and bounced on his haunches, thumping the ground. The paramedic stood up, looking as if he might run. Gerry's father gripped the man's forearm.

"Just stay calm. We have to stand together. Look it right in the eye. Don't look away."

"I don't know—"

"I *do*," said his father.

They stood there just staring at Gerry. Slowly, his anger subsided. He found himself pacing in a slow circle, grunting. It was as if he had no choice in the matter. Gradually, the rage fogging his brain cleared and he was able to think again. This wasn't doing him any good. He turned his back on the men and walked off. When he was a short distance away, he stopped and sat down in the grass.

"It's all right," he heard his father say. "I don't think it will bother us now." The paramedic returned his attention to Gerry's human body while his father stood nearby.

The other paramedic left his mother, who was lying on the grass, and told the men, "She's stable. But I think we should get both of them to the hospital at Kondoa as soon as possible."

His father went over and knelt beside her. Gerry was too far away to hear what they were saying, but he saw him hold her hand and at one point he thought he heard his mother crying. He wanted, somehow, to tell them he was...what? That he was all right? He was not all right. But he was alive. And he was not in pain. He wanted to go to them but he knew that his approach would only make things worse. There was nothing he could do.

The paramedics spent a long time working over his body, listening to his heart with the stethoscope. They straightened his leg and inflated a splint around it. They talked to someone on a radio and then they brought a stretcher and put his body on it and carried it into the ambulance. After a while, Gerry's mother was able to stand, and his father helped her into the ambulance, too.

One of the paramedics climbed into the wreckage of the plane and came out a short time later, stripping a rubber glove from his hand. There was blood on it.

He closed the back doors to the ambulance and then got in. They moved slowly, keeping the pitching of the van to a minimum as they drove back toward the road. It would be little more than a pair of rutted tracks at this time of year and the driver would have to look hard to find it.

Gerry could not see the road from where he sat, but suddenly the ambulance was no longer bouncing. It turned and picked up speed, moving straight and level. He heard the electronic yodel of its siren and watched its flashing lights disappear over the restless arches of grass. For a while, he stood on his haunches so that he could follow it for a little longer.

Then he sat down again. He listened to the siren for as long as he could, until it was lost in the wind ruffling the grass.

And then there was only the veldt, rolling to the horizon.

THE LEOPARD

The troop had moved on. In the distance, he saw them, dark humps rising and falling as they traveled through the yellow grass. One of them, maybe it was Hector, kept turning around to see if Gerry was following. But he did not want to be with the baboons. The *other* baboons.

How could this happen? The paramedic said he was still alive. If his body wasn't dead, then neither was he. This wasn't some kind of afterlife. And if the paramedics had only given him oxygen, then he couldn't be hallucinating on drugs. Unless, of course, they really had given him drugs and he'd only hallucinated that they gave him oxygen. It was becoming easier to just believe what his senses were telling him: he was inside a baboon's body, as surely as if he had been born a monkey.

Gerry turned away from the troop to the wreckage of the plane. He found himself drawn to it. He started toward the cockpit in a trot and was again surprised by the ease with which he covered the ground. He went over to the door and put his paw on the latch. This was strangest of all, seeing a furry arm ending in a black hand gripping the latch, and knowing it was his. The paramedic had done his best to close the door to the cabin on leaving, but it didn't quite fit anymore. One of the hinges was no longer attached to the wall, which had crumpled during the crash. Gerry pulled on the door and it creaked open.

Inside the cabin, most of the seats were still anchored to the floor. It took Gerry a moment to realize that only the ones that had been occupied were missing—the added weight of their bodies had torn them loose. Gerry and his mother must have flown out through the hole in the roof or the open rear cargo door. During the crash, the plane had spun around and now this opening was blocked with a section of the ramp and a mound of dirt and branches.

Gerry turned to the cockpit, which was separated from the passenger cabin by the backs of the seats and a short riser.

Sunlight streamed in through the windshield, and the buzzing of flies filled the sweltering cockpit. From where he stood, he could see that the pilot's seat had come loose from the floor and had smashed forward into the instrument panel and the windshield. Or maybe the nose of the plane had been crushed into the chair. Stan's headset had come off during the impact and was lying on the floor. Gerry looked at the light green ear cups with the word "Roberts" and the arrowed logo on each of them. Every pilot seemed to wear the same type of headset.

Roberts.

He could still read the word.

Seven times seven is forty-nine.

Twelve-twenty-six Wellwyn Avenue.

He still had Gerry Copeland's memories and thoughts. So his mind couldn't be physically occupying a baboon's brain, could it? Didn't a person need the machinery of their brain to do the things that people do, like read and open door latches and do arithmetic? How could he be thinking like a human being if he no longer had a human being's body?

He could see the back of Stan's head. Flies were landing on his crewcut and struggling through the bristles at the crown to bite at his scalp. Gerry didn't want to see his face. The bloody crater in the windshield told him all he wanted to know about that. He remembered that he didn't like Stan much, and felt a stab of guilt.

"Going into town for a few beers are we?" he'd say to Gerry as he helped him onto the plane. "Just nipping out for a little skirt?"

He supposed Stan thought it was funny. But when neither Gerry nor his parents ever laughed, you'd have thought he'd give it up—after the fourth or fifth time. But no, Gerry had to endure the stupid ritual every time they got onto the plane.

He knew it was dumb, but he was going to miss wincing over Stan's lame joke. He wanted, more than anything at that moment, to hear a human voice.

It occurred to Gerry that they would have to come back for the body. Maybe Dad would be with them. If Gerry stayed here, he might be able to tell him, somehow, who he was. If he could show him he was Gerry...what? What could his father possibly do? He needed to think.

Gerry looked around the ruin of the cockpit. He didn't want to stay here. It was too hot, and more and more flies were finding their way in through the open door. Gerry turned from the cockpit and moved down the narrow aisle of the passenger cabin. Stan had once showed him where the survival kit was stowed. It contained water and rations. He found it near the cargo ramp—a latched, metal box like a first aid kit that was strapped to the wall. He braced his thumbs under the latches and pushed. Nothing happened. His arms might be strong, but apparently his thumbs were weak compared to a boy's. He pushed harder and this time one of the latches snapped open. Then the other.

Inside the box were flares, a compass, flint, and what he most wanted: a can of water and a block of survival food. Gerry saw that the expiry date had passed three years ago. Thanks, Stan.

He had some trouble with the pull tab on the water can, but finally got a fingernail under it.

He put the can to his mouth and drank. He spilled quite a bit of it at first. It took him a few tries to seal the rim of the can with his monkey lips. The water was warm and had an odd, dusty taste, like water left sitting in a glass too long. The block of survival food wasn't heavy, but it was too big for him to grip in one hand. He had to cradle it against his body. He had no way of carrying the other supplies.

He went out into the brightness of the savanna again and tried to close the door behind him. He struggled with it for a full minute before he asked himself why. *You're a monkey, and you're trying to close a door behind you. What's the point? So that flies won't bite Stan?*

He pushed the thought away because he didn't even want to know what would happen if he tried laughing. It was the kind of thing his parents might have discussed over dinner. Can baboons laugh?

The sun would soon be setting. He knew enough about baboons to know that they didn't like to be on the ground after dark, and that they had reason. He started toward the acacia he had awakened under earlier. He moved on three legs, clutching the survival food with his free paw.

A fly buzzed around him, and he caught a green, metallic flash in the slanting rays of the sun. The day was already starting to cool off, and he wondered if he would be cold tonight.

Reaching the tree, he was again thrilled by the ease with which he climbed it—even with one hand occupied by the block of food. His fingers found every ridge and strip in the bark and he just pulled himself upward. He willed it and it happened. It was exhilarating! Reaching the first thick branch was easy. After that, the bark became smoother and getting a grip was a little more difficult, but he could now grab individual branches. He hooked the hand holding the block of food over a limb and pulled himself into the thick of the tree. There he found the crotch of a branch that seemed to fit his back, and he settled in against it.

As the darkness gathered, he studied the package.

There were various helpful messages written on it. "Will not increase thirst," was displayed in the largest type. That was reassuring. He tore the wrapping from the survival food and sniffed. It smelled faintly nutty. He began gnawing on the block and found that it was a little like nougat, only harder and less sweet. Food only the desperate could appreciate. He wondered if they made it that way deliberately, so that people wouldn't eat it during better times.

If being a baboon wasn't an emergency, he didn't know what was.

As he chiseled at the block with his incisors, his skull resonated with the scraping sound. He stopped when he thought he heard something. And then a different smell filled his nostrils, and he felt the hairs along his shoulders and the back of his neck stand up. It was as if something ancient, the veldt itself, had breathed on him. Some part of his mind knew that smell, and it filled him with fear.

Gerry first saw the leopard as a shadow flowing from bush to rock to tree, but always toward him, as surely as if he were drinking that liquid dark. As a compass needle seeks north, it came to him. And it filled him with such fear that he screamed. He tried to cram back the sound but it seemed as natural and as right to scream as anything he had done in his life. It was the baboon alarm call, warning the rest of the troop that the enemy was here.

Only there was no troop; there was only him, and that was why the leopard was coming.

And now it reached the base of the tree. Gerry saw the gliding of its shoulder blades beneath its pelt as it advanced then rose up the trunk as smoothly as if there had been no change in direction at all. It drew closer as if it were reeling Gerry in by the acacia's trunk, toward the jaws that would end his life with one, precise bite to the nape of his neck. And so Gerry moved, climbing higher, clawing his way through the crackling branches, grateful for the cape of fur protecting his neck and shoulders.

Still the leopard came without a sound. It was like being pursued by a shadow. Only now, as they emerged into the moonlight at the top of the tree, Gerry could see the rings of its yellow eyes.

The branch thinned as Gerry moved toward the tip, until he could almost encircle it with his fingers. It began to sag under his weight, and the weight of the cat as it followed him. Gerry looked down. It was easily twenty feet to the ground. The fall probably wouldn't kill him, but if he broke a bone, he knew that it would be over for him.

Now the leopard was slowing, as there was very little for its claws to grip. Gerry managed to increase the distance between them by about an arm's length. The branch sagged farther as he moved outward.

He realized he now had the advantage. He pushed off with his legs and swung from the branch by his hands—a hairy, screaming Christmas ornament. The branch sprang upward, nearly unbalancing the cat. It growled in reaction, and Gerry yanked down again, trying to catch the momentum of the swing. The leopard backed up, trying to get its claws into thicker branches, and nearly fell again. It was working!

Then, with a sickening crunch, Gerry's branch broke—but

not completely. Gripping only a strip of peeling bark, he swung down and reached out for a second, lower branch. He snagged it with his free hand and the branch bowed, lowering him another six or seven feet. Gerry released it, hitting the ground at a run.

It would only take the leopard a second to turn around and head down the tree. Gerry ran over the tufts of grass, silvered by moonlight, toward the ruined plane.

He ran for his life, pulling in the space between himself and the plane. When he was almost there, he dared turn and he saw the leopard as it poured silently down the trunk of the tree and into the grass.

Gerry reached the cabin door and yanked on the handle and it barely budged. Again, and this time it scraped open a few inches, enough for him to force his legs and hips inside. As he struggled to pull his shoulders through the opening, he saw the cat coming toward him, a mottled streak, and with a last effort he squeezed inside and grabbed the door handle. The door was too bent to latch so he braced his legs on the bulkhead and pulled for all he was worth just as the leopard threw itself against the door with a thud. Gerry held fast and listened to the pounding and scraping of the leopard's paws as it leaped against the metal.

Then the scraping sounds stopped and were replaced by a low growling which circled away, then came near again. Gerry pictured the cat pacing outside the door. There was another brief scratching of claws on metal, and then quiet. After a long time he heard nothing at all but the hammering of his heart in his ears, but he kept on gripping the handle until his hands ached.

For hours, he watched a bar of moonlight creep up the wall and then fragment into the shadows of tree branches before fading altogether. The moon was setting.

Still he clung to the door. Even when he dared to let go, he stayed inside the plane. He went into the cockpit and hopped onto the co-pilot's seat. He put his forepaws on the instrument panel and looked out through the windshield. Now that the moon had set, it was too dark to see anything except for ribbons of grass and the faint outline of the acacia tree against the starry sky.

The pilot was draped over the control column, his white shirt glowing faintly in the darkness. Sharing the cabin with Stan's body was the last thing he wanted…no, make that the second-to-last thing. The last thing he wanted, he was now quite certain, was to be eaten by a leopard.

He would wait until they returned for the body. They couldn't leave their friend here, his face all blood and glass and part of an instrument panel. Gerry was certain his father wouldn't allow such a thing. In the morning, he would come for it. And then Gerry would have to find some way to communicate with his father.

HE HAD NEVER BEEN SO GLAD OF A SUNRISE IN HIS LIFE. As soon as the first rays began picking out the dew, he pushed open the cockpit door just far enough to poke his head out. Nothing but wet grass. In an hour, it would be dry. He scrambled on top of the wreck and looked in the direction he had seen the ambulance take the day before. He could barely make out the dry ruts, nearly overgrown.

He watched the progress of the sun, and concentrated on the horizon. *What if they don't come?*

He couldn't spend another night here. Stan's body was beginning to smell. He knew that if he could smell it as strongly as he did, now, others—with senses far keener than his own—would already be coming. Long before nightfall, the scent would bring more than the leopard. Daytime predators would come scavenging. How long could he wait inside the cabin, hanging onto the door handle, growing weaker by the hour?

By noon, he began to doubt that his father was coming. He had to make a decision: stay another night in the Skyvan with Stan's body, or find some other shelter. He was not defenseless. He was strong and fast. His canines were fearsome weapons. But they would not save him from a pride of lions or a pack of hyenas. Trees would protect him from these predators, but not the leopard. And it would be back tonight, hunting for him.

Gerry also knew that a baboon traveling alone on the savanna was taking a risk. But a lone baboon knowing nothing about where to find food and water would soon be in serious trouble—even if he were lucky enough to avoid any predators.

Gradually, he realized that there was only one choice open to him if he were going to survive. He was going to have to find the troop.

He looked around him at a landscape both strange and familiar. He had last seen them moving toward a dark spot—there, about three quarters of the way to the horizon, trembling in the heat. Even with his keen eyes, it was hard to tell what it was at this distance. Probably just a big rock.

He knew that each day his parents followed the troop from their sleeping rocks to their foraging grounds and back again. And yet he had not seen the baboons return last night. They probably moved in a circuit, rather than doubling back along a line. But if that were true, wouldn't he have seen them this morning? It was possible they passed the plane and he had missed them. Or maybe they had caught the leopard's scent and stayed away.

The baboons had their own scent. If Gerry could smell it, then he could follow them. All he had to do was cross their path. But would he know the scent when he found it? Gerry sniffed his own arm. It didn't smell like anything to him. But even if he couldn't smell himself, surely he could smell other baboons.

Gerry set off in the direction he had last seen them. Whether he would recognize their scent or not, he didn't know. But he was sure of one thing: the leopard could pick up his. And this time there would be no plane in which to hide.

He had until nightfall to find them.

THE TROOP

Midday, and Gerry's shadow shrank beneath him. Like a thing alive, it sought the shade. But the troop would be resting this time of day, so now was his best chance to catch up with them. As he walked, he found that the cape of hair covering his head and shoulders, which Gerry had always imagined would be hot, was quite the opposite. It was much cooler than the exposed skin on his snout and rump.

After an hour's walking, he estimated that he was halfway to the dark spot, which he saw now was definitely a rock, maybe as big as a house. Here, he detected what he thought was the troop's scent—a mix of hair and sweat. It could be any animal, but he continued in the same direction, and he thought that the scent grew stronger. Or maybe it was just his imagination. The variety of smells he inhaled with every breath was bewildering. He knew now that his sense of smell as a person had been a pale ghost of what other mammals experienced.

His human mind was overwhelmed by what his baboon nose brought to it now. He was drowning in odors, and longed for a breath of fresh air. Except that this *was* fresh air. Under other circumstances the perfume of a hundred plant and animal species might have been inviting, but right now they only distracted him as he tried to concentrate on one, the baboon odor. Just as he thought he was able to grasp it, it wafted away, wrapped in a dozen other scents.

Out in the open he felt exposed, and not only to the heat. His main worry was the lions and hyenas, and the grass here was tall enough to conceal them. He stopped often and turned downwind. This was the direction from which a predator was most likely to approach, and they had no way of knowing that Gerry could hardly tell one smell from another. But he had smelled the leopard the night before; some part of his baboon brain had recognized its odor long before he had seen or heard it.

It took him much longer than he had thought it would to reach the big outcrop of rock—a great, black loaf of lava surrounded by grass. Not that he could really be sure how much time had passed. Gerry wanted to laugh when he found himself glancing at his left wrist. He had always worn a watch, and he still checked it often. Nothing but hair there now.

He was thirsty. Gerry circled the rock, hoping to find some trace of water, or at least a little shade. He found a shadow beneath a horn of rock at the base just big enough for him to huddle in. But the black rock radiated so much heat that it was almost worse than being in the direct sunlight.

He watched a little green bee eater land on the bare branch of a tree that had struggled out of a crack in the rock and died. The bird was maybe half a city block away, but Gerry could see a wasp pinched in the tweezers of its slender beak. The bee eater scraped off the wasp's stinger on the branch and then swallowed the wriggling insect.

They sat watching each other for a little while. The bird's plumage was a brilliant green, with an iridescence that Gerry didn't recall seeing with his old eyes. Then the bee eater flew off, and Gerry started out again.

He walked for what seemed like hours under the lengthening light of the afternoon, drifting from the track of the baboon smell, stopping, sniffing, and starting again.

He caught sight of them feeding late in the day. Some of the male baboons interrupted their foraging and turned toward him. They didn't seem alarmed, but they definitely took notice.

Gerry continued to close the distance between them, foraging for food as he went. The problem was, he didn't know what they were eating. At this distance it was impossible to see through the grass, but they were picking through the soil for something. That was another reason that Gerry needed to join the troop. From his parents' conversations, he knew that baboons ate a huge variety of foods—mainly bugs and parts of various plants. He could probably even recall most of the plant and insect names that he had heard his parents use. The problem was that he couldn't identify those plants by sight. And the wrong choice here could be deadly; there was no shortage of poisonous plants and animals in Africa.

Gerry did his best to imitate the baboons' movements, working his way closer. One by one—almost as if taking turns—the others glanced up at him, and then just as quickly resumed scrabbling at the soil. He soon realized that he must have been a familiar member of the troop; no one seemed to notice that he had been away at all. After a short time spent picking his way toward the others, he was close enough to recognize individual troop members.

There was Sphinx, a young male whose attention could be held by the simplest of objects. They called him Sphinx because he would often adopt a curious lion-like pose: resting on his belly, head erect, with his forepaws stretched out in front of him like the ancient monument. He would sit like this for hours, studying some perfectly ordinary stone or tree or puddle. Once, when Gerry had accompanied his mother into the field, they had watched him stare, transfixed, at a termite mound for a full hour. Later, after the troop had moved on, Gerry approached the mound to see what the monkey had been staring at, but as far as he could tell there was nothing remarkable about it.

By now Gerry had worked his way past the margins of the troop. He needed to get close enough to at least one other baboon to see what it was eating without intruding on its foraging space. So far, so good.

The only adult member of the troop who displayed open interest in Gerry was an old male with a hunched posture that gave him a somewhat servile appearance. Gerry didn't remember seeing him before, but decided to call him Chet.

Chet solved Gerry's problem of getting closer to the troop when he ambled over and stood right next to him. But Chet wasn't foraging—instead he seemed to take a keen interest in Gerry's every move. Chet reminded him of a waiter in a fancy French restaurant who paid just a little too much attention to one of his diners. *And how are the seed pods today, monsieur? Not too ripe, I hope. Is everything to your liking?* All Chet needed was a napkin draped over his arm. Gerry couldn't decide whether to shoo him away or give him a tip.

A baboon his parents called Mavis stole glances in Gerry's direction. She was still carrying Oscar, an infant who rode around on her back like a jockey on a horse. Mavis's high rank had long been a mystery to Gerry's parents, and they had spent many hours puzzling over her. For a female baboon, rank was usually determined by family. Being born into a high-ranking family meant getting the best food, the most comfortable sleeping places, and attracting the largest and strongest males. Somehow, Mavis had become one of the troop's dominant females despite being born into a low-ranking family. While her weaker sisters were hounded and pushed around by all but the youngest members of the troop, Mavis was respected. No one would have known they were sisters if Gerry's parents hadn't sampled their DNA.

Oscar enjoyed all of the benefits of his privileged birth. Full of his mother's milk, he was bold and playful—and very curious about Gerry. He hopped from his saddle onto the grass, but before he could get anywhere near Gerry, Mavis scooped him up again.

Zeus was the troop's dominant male. Apart from his size, his top rank was apparent from the large, empty area surrounding him. All the other baboons were careful not to intrude on his space while he was feeding.

Zeus barely looked over at Gerry before returning to his foraging. The others—fully forty of them—each took their turn to glance at him, but no one made a move. Gerry tried to see what it was they were eating. He moved closer until he was just a few lengths away from another baboon.

He had thought that it must be grubs of some kind, but whatever it was, it was actively trying to escape the baboons, who were digging as fast as they could to keep up. It looked like hard work—baboons' hands are not good digging tools as their fingers have nails like a person's, rather than claws.

He watched Zeus pluck one of the creatures from the grass and bring it struggling to his mouth. The baboon bit the animal's head off, and then it was still, giving Gerry his first good look at it. The creature was pink and hairless and about the size of a rat. Now that it was dead, Zeus was able to finish it at his leisure. Gerry tried to puzzle out what it was without staring too obviously. Except for the lack of hair, it looked like a rodent. The only thing Gerry could think of that would fit the description would be a naked mole rat. He had never seen one before, but he knew they stayed underground in colonies with a single breeding queen—living more like ants or bees than mammals.

The sound of its bones crunching was nauseating. Well, it should have been nauseating, but perhaps baboons didn't get nauseated. Gerry felt nothing.

He watched the other members of the troop. Every now and then they seemed to stop and watch for some sign before resuming their frantic digging. Or were they listening?

A young male baboon wandered closer, ignoring Gerry. It was Hector. He watched the ground at Gerry's feet and suddenly a tiny spray of earth erupted from the grass, quickly forming a cone of fresh earth. Hector plunged one hand and then the other into the volcano, digging until he uncovered a rat-like tail and a pair of scrabbling back feet. He dragged out the struggling mole rat. It tried to swing around and bite the monkey's hand with its enormous, chisel-like incisors, but in one deft motion the baboon bit off its head, just as Zeus had. Then he brushed the earth from the wrinkly body and chomped into it with that terrible crunching sound. In an instant, it was swallowed and gone. Hector smacked his lips and Gerry could have sworn he was grinning at him.

Gerry was still looking at Hector when a second mole hill erupted from the soil. Hector looked from the little volcano to Gerry as if to ask, "Yours?" and Gerry knew that if he did not take it, it would look strange. Gerry plunged in with his hands, scraping away the earth behind the retreating mole rat as fast as he could, exposing its tail and the churning pink legs. He grabbed them and pulled out the squirming rodent. As he fought for the courage to bite into it, the animal twisted back and bit Gerry and he dropped it. Before he realized what he was doing, Gerry smashed the mole rat into the grass with his fist. The second time he hit it, it was still. Gerry looked up and saw that the entire troop was watching, waiting for him to collect his reward.

Avoiding the ugly head with the monstrous incisors, Gerry reached down, picked up the animal, and, hesitating only for a second, crammed it tail-first into his mouth. He had thought the crunching sound of its bones was bad when Hector and Zeus ate theirs; inside his own head the noise was ten times worse. Crunch. Crunch. Crunch.

The taste was meaty, yet it had a curious tang to it—almost like mustard. It was delicious, and Gerry was reminded how badly he needed food. He looked over at the troop, feeling something like gratitude, but they had already returned to their own foraging. Gerry listened and probed the soil for a while longer, until he noticed that Zeus had started moving again. The rest of the troop straggled after him.

As he started to follow the troop, something tiny shot through the grass ahead of Gerry and into the shade of a whistling thorn tree. It was probably another mole rat, flushed from a burrow by one of the others. Gerry raced after it at, but something slammed into him with such force that it sent him rolling. He struggled to get his legs under him again and saw a large and very solid-looking baboon also pick himself up from the grass, shake his head, and look directly at him.

This was not good. Primates didn't stare directly at one another except in anger. He recognized this brute from one of the days he had accompanied his parents into the field. They had named him Lothar, and Gerry remembered disliking this animal even after seeing him only through binoculars.

Now he stood right in front of Gerry, chest thrust out, his cape bristling. His lips did not quite close properly on one side of his muzzle, giving him a perpetual snarl. Even without the snarl, Gerry had the impression that he would not look pleased.

Gerry avoided eye contact, but Lothar wasn't having any of it. He yawned, drawing his lips back from the yellow canines. He also flashed his eye patches—white blotches on his eyelids. By raising its eyebrows and partially closing its eyes, a baboon displays these patches, and its anger. Gerry slowly backed up a few steps, trying to make the movement as casual as he could. In a moment, Lothar was going to charge.

The last thing Gerry needed was a fight. But he had two choices: keep his place in the troop or end up in the belly of the leopard. It wasn't much of a choice. Even if he stayed with the troop but was bloodied in a fight, the leopard might still find him. He decided that he would run if he had to.

But when Lothar came rolling toward him, roaring, Gerry barked and stood his ground. It was like when his father threw the rock at him: he just did it. Startled, Lothar stopped, but then he charged again. He kept flanking Gerry, looking for a place to sink his teeth. Gerry scrambled to face him, barking and roaring. Lothar seemed confused by Gerry's response, and clearly expected him to run. Maybe the baboon whose body Gerry now occupied always ran.

Gerry retreated about twenty feet, but didn't dare turn his back on the baboon. Lothar beat the ground with his hands and barked, but came no closer. It seemed this was enough for the moment. Eventually, Lothar returned his attention to the search for food, moving in the direction of the others. Gerry foraged with them until sunset, but his first mole rat was also his last for that day.

THEY MOVED HOMEWARD AS THEY GRAZED and, as the sun rolled down the western sky, the sleeping rocks rose like a set of emergent molars—first from the horizon, and then from the ground around them. The outcrop, as tall as a five-story building and shaped "like a giant tea cozy" as Gerry's mother once put it, was almost naked of vegetation. On a hot day, staying on the rocks would have been unbearable. Apart from the heat, there was nothing to eat or drink. But at night, as the stone gave back its heat to the night air, the baboons welcomed the warmth. More important, the rocks were too steep for a leopard or a lion to climb. The monkeys, with their grasping hands, held the advantage here.

Gerry wanted only to be out of the leopard's reach, but the troop loitered around a pond at the base of the rocks, resting and grooming one another while the infants played—racing in and out of the trees as the sun brushed the grass in streaks of pink. After a while, the baboons started taking turns drinking at the pond.

Then, as a bird folds its wings, darkness gathered.

Zeus started the long climb to the top of the rocks, picking his way along a path the troop had always followed. A baboon might live thirty years, but how long a troop lasted, with members born into it and dying out of it, nobody knew. His father had said, "Maybe centuries. Maybe longer."

One at a time, the rest of the baboons followed Zeus while Gerry kept glancing to the trees, awaiting his turn. But the others did not seem the least bit nervous. Gerry waited for the last of the troop to ascend before he, too, started up the rock face, feeling its heat in his palms and the soles of his feet. He tried to keep track of Lothar's place in the line, and knew that he was somewhere near the head, now far up the cliff face. In the gathering dark, Gerry could just make out the shape of a big male against the sky. Gerry had the definite impression that he had stopped climbing and was looking down at him. He seemed to be waiting while the others climbed past. If it was Lothar, Gerry knew that with the advantages of both size and higher ground, it would be easy to push Gerry down the rock face. He stopped and looked around at the darkening plain behind him. When he looked up again, whoever waited on the rocks above was gone. Something told him to go no farther.

There was a narrow ledge to his left, blocked by a bulge in the cliff face. Gerry hugged the rock and edged around to it, then sat back on his haunches. He would sleep here tonight.

It was far from an ideal spot. Anything tracking the troop's scent would first encounter Gerry, and Gerry alone. Still, he was far enough above the veldt that he could watch for any predator coming for him, and it would not be easy for a leopard to get past that last bulge.

At the summit above him, the troop found their places and began the nightly ritual of grooming as the last daylight fled the sky.

Gerry found a hollow in the rock and leaned into it. It was hard, but the heat rising through the stone felt good. Perhaps, if he returned to the downed plane, he could find a blanket. He closed his eyes and listened to the grunting and lip-smacking from the rocks above.

Strangely, even more than wishing he wasn't a baboon, he wished that he could tell someone about it. Dear Milton: Today I ate a mole rat.

You what? Why...?

Everyone was doing it. I was just trying to fit in.

I told you this would happen.

When? When did you ever tell me I would turn into a baboon?

I told you you would grow up weird if you hung around those animals for too long.

Okay. Maybe he wouldn't tell Milton. Someone else. Someone who wouldn't blame him for what had happened, because Gerry was pretty sure it wasn't his fault. Still, it had happened to him. And he'd never heard of anything like this happening to anyone else. There had to be a reason.

He kept thinking of eating the mole rat. The mustard tang of its flesh and the crunching of its tiny bones came back to him. It was disgusting, but at the same time, his mouth watered at the thought. He'd eat another one right now, if he could.

LIFE AT THE BOTTOM

Gerry dreamed he was in Croydon, in a cold room under crisp sheets. He dreaded the thought of exposing himself to that cold, of leaving his warm bed and showering and choosing a shirt and going to school. Mixed with the smell of laundry soap was that of coffee percolating from downstairs, and the sounds of his mother moving about the kitchen: he heard the rush of kibble sliding down the cardboard chute of its almost empty box and the tinkling as it hit the cat's bowl. Water drumming in a steel sink. The growl of the garbage disposal.

In a moment he would will himself to open his eyes. He would see the straight lines and right angles of his bedroom: the door frame. His desk. His dresser drawers in their orderly rows.

But when he opened his eyes he was looking at a pattern of cracks in the rock he was sleeping on.

His arm was asleep.

Gerry sat up and felt a cold tingling as blood returned to the limb. The moment the distraction left, he was aware of hunger gnawing at him. He had to find more to eat today, or he would soon be too weak to keep up with the troop. The sun had just cleared the horizon and the baboons were clambering past him on their way down from their stone beds.

Good, thought Gerry. Finding food would be the first order of the day. He looked down from his ledge and saw Mavis leading the procession. She was followed by two other high-ranking females, including her daughter, Sophie, and another baboon Gerry didn't recognize. Then came Zeus. Although Zeus was the largest of all the baboons—larger, even, than Lothar—his age was showing. Each of his movements seemed an effort, especially now, first thing in the morning. Gerry wondered how much longer he could hold the top place. A troop's highest-ranking male held the position only for as long as he could win a fight against any of the other males—or, at least, for as long as nobody else dared to challenge him. But the other big males, like Lothar, must have noticed how slowly the old king moved. Sooner or later, someone would test his leadership.

As Zeus lowered himself past the ledge where Gerry had slept, he turned and looked directly at him for a moment with his big, watery eyes. It was not a challenging look, although Gerry was careful to glance away. But in the second their eyes met, the old baboon seemed to appraise Gerry. *What are you doing all the way down here?* he seemed to ask. But by the time Gerry looked back, he had started down the last of the rock slope toward the trees.

Gerry saw scars on the back of Zeus's neck and shoulders—hairless furrows raked over his shoulder blades. They were old, from long before Gerry's parents had begun observing the troop. Gerry's father had guessed that they were probably from a lion. Somehow, Zeus had survived a lion attack. One look at those scars would make most baboons think long and hard before applying for Zeus's job—especially, thought Gerry, if that baboon had been around to witness the original battle.

Or was it possible, he wondered, that they just respected him?

Next was Oscar, riding Rhona, one of his mother's close female friends. Oscar was the young one who had wanted to come to him the day before. Gerry wondered if he had played with Oscar in the past. By "he," he meant the baboon body that he had entered a few days ago. Gerry had been trying to picture that baboon in his mind and recall if his mother and father had assigned him a name. He wished that he'd paid more attention when he was in the field with his parents. If he could recall that baboon, he would have a better idea of where his place was within the troop—although he was getting a pretty good idea already.

But as he watched the baboons gather by the pond at the base of the sleeping rocks, he was able to match only a few of them to monkeys he had watched in the field. From listening to his parents, he knew more names, but he didn't know the animals that went with them.

Who was *he*? If only he had a mirror. It might help him to remember.

The others ringed the pool to drink, and as they bent to the water their bare and rosy bums faced outward to moon the savanna. Gerry would have laughed if he could. They took turns dipping their heads to the water while a few stood watch. Suddenly, Gerry realized he could look at his reflection in the pool. Without thinking, he dashed toward the troop.

Just then, Lothar raised his head.

He glanced across the shallow pond and barked at Gerry, causing the others to scatter and look around in panic. Zeus looked from Lothar to Gerry. Seeing it was only a false alarm, he splashed into the pond and cuffed Lothar, who retreated, grumbling and flashing his eye patches. Lothar also yawned at Gerry, exposing his huge canines—another show of aggression.

By the time Lothar was far enough from the pond for Gerry to move in and take a drink, the water looked like coffee with milk. The troop was moving on and he gulped down as much of the brown water as he could and then leaned over the surface, waiting for the fragments of his reflection to assemble as the water calmed again. What he saw shocked him—not that he was a baboon, but that he was such a scrawny one. He was a young male, no more than five years old, but his fur was patchy and his limbs thin. Life had not been easy for him. And yet many of the others in the troop appeared sleek and healthy. Clearly, there was food to be had. Gerry could only conclude that he was far from the top of the troop's pecking order. Climbing any higher was going to be difficult with this body.

How hard soon became clear to him, as he caught up with the troop. They had stopped beneath a patchy canopy of acacia trees to dig for something. Gerry sidled up next to a female and her nursing daughter and watched.

With quick movements of her fingers, she was digging around a clump of grass, clearing away the dirt. Gerry imitated her digging. The soil was moist and loose here. But the stringy clump of roots didn't look like much of a meal.

Gerry looked again at the female's excavation. Her little hands moved so quickly that it was hard to tell exactly what she was doing. After a moment he realized that it wasn't the roots she was after, but the underground runner connecting one clump of grass to the next. He got a good look at it when she pulled up the runner, brushed the dirt from it by rubbing it on the fur of her upper arm, and popped it into her mouth. And then she was on to the next clump of grass.

It took Gerry a long time to uncover his runner, but when he finally worked it free of the soil and stuck it into his mouth, it was juicy and almost sweet.

But it was like eating one bean sprout. It would take dozens—maybe hundreds—to make a meal. Gerry looked up at the rest of the troop, hunched over their work, and shrugged to himself. He guessed this was how it was done.

He moved on to his next clump of grass and began working at the soil around the roots. As he dug, a large male came and stood next to him. But he wasn't digging. Instead, he just glanced from Gerry to the trees above them and back again. Maybe this guy was hoping to pick up a few pointers, too. It took Gerry a few minutes to clear the soil from around the root and he had decided it was just clear enough to pluck it free when the baboon next to him began yawning and flashing his eye patches. Gerry just stared at him. *What's your problem?* Suddenly, the bigger male gave a loud bark and shoved Gerry hard. Gerry picked himself up off the ground and turned back toward the baboon in time to see it pull up the runner and eat it. Then he just stood there, chewing, with his eyes fixed on Gerry.

Right. So that's how it works around here.

Gerry moved off and found another clump of grass, but he could see the other baboon watching him as he started digging. Gerry had the runner about half uncovered when the other baboon sidled up to him again.

Gerry stopped and just stared at the bully.

Wrong move.

The baboon lunged at him and in a moment it was standing over Gerry with its jaws around his neck. Gerry kept as still as he could, but there seemed nothing he could do to keep a pathetic yelping sound from rising in his throat, over and over. It was humiliating. But whatever was making him do it, it eventually seemed to satisfy the other baboon, who let him up and, as if to make his point absolutely clear, plucked the runner from the ground and, again, ate it.

This time, Gerry kept his eyes averted as the other baboon stood over him.

He was beginning to see why he was so scrawny. Gerry retreated to a place beyond the canopy of the trees. It seemed too much effort for the bully to follow him. Instead, he began picking on some other poor sap, a female about Gerry's age.

But the ground here was harder than it was directly under the trees, and Gerry had to dig much longer to uncover each runner, and they weren't nearly as juicy as the one he had eaten before.

Gerry looked at the others foraging a little ways off and realized that he had another, more serious, problem: he was at the fringes of the troop. If that leopard or anything else came around looking for a baboon to eat, Gerry might as well have "special of the day" stamped on his forehead. Not, he reminded himself, that he really had a forehead anymore. But that was always who the predators went for—the skinny guy at the edge of the pack.

His choices were grim: forage with the troop and have almost everything he worked for eaten by bullies, or forage without the troop and risk being eaten himself.

HE FINISHED THE DAY EXHAUSTED and hardly less hungry than when he had started. His fingers ached so much from digging that he could hardly grip the nubs and crevices in the sleeping rocks well enough to climb them. The day's only success was learning one more food that a baboon could eat: grass runners.

Like the night before, he slept away from the others. Lying on his bed of stone, he could hear the soft grunts and lip smacking of baboons at peace. If any of it had been directed at him, he might have taken some comfort in the sounds.

Each day brought a new mix of terror and humiliation. About a week after his first run-in with one of the troop's endless supply of bullies, they followed a small herd of elephants into a grove of fever trees. While the elephants tore bark from the trees for reasons unclear to Gerry, the troop followed, picking at the exposed sap. The gum had very little taste or odor to Gerry, but the baboons went after it with almost frenzied enthusiasm, picking up as much of it as they could with their fingers. The elephants largely ignored the baboons, who ate around the destruction.

But Gerry learned the hard way that they were tolerated only as long as they stayed well away from the elephants' babies. He wandered too near a calf and the mother grabbed Gerry by the leg with her trunk and flung him into the branches of the fever tree. He was only bruised, but the elephant might just as easily have beat him against the ground. That was the end of sap-eating for the troop that day, which did nothing to endear Gerry to them. For two days, Chet was the only other baboon who would come near him—except, of course, for Lothar, who still took every opportunity to pick on him.

And so the days went. Gerry did his best to observe and learn from the others, but the baboons communicated in so many ways that it was hard to keep up with their varied and subtle signals.

HE LEARNED ONE THING, THOUGH: for years, he had listened to his parents talk about one baboon "presenting" to another, but had never given much thought to what it really meant. From the way they used the word, he had always assumed that it was some sign of respect. He had pictured one baboon bowing to another, or saluting, or perhaps bringing it a dead mouse or some other little gift. But he now realized that presenting meant approaching whomever it was you wanted to impress, turning your back on him, and sticking your bum in his face. So he had almost had it right: it was a bit like bowing, only in the wrong direction.

Presenting, he was learning, was a way of apologizing, begging, or just wishing someone a pleasant good morning.

Needless to say, no one was doing any presenting to Gerry.

But presenting was something he planned to do a lot of. He was looking forward to telling the troop, one by one, to kiss his rosy bum.

He took some comfort in realizing, gradually, that there were plenty of other baboons who were picked on. In fact, most of the monkeys in the troop were pushed around by someone. It was nothing personal.

The only baboon who seemed to exist outside the pecking order was Sphinx. One day, Gerry saw him staring down a… well, Gerry wasn't exactly sure what it was. It might have been a bush, or something *in* the bush. Sometimes you couldn't tell what he was looking at. Whatever it was, he just sat there in the Sphinx pose, staring straight ahead. Lothar came by and sat down next to him—Sphinx's signal to leave. But Sphinx just kept staring. Lothar's hostility escalated through all the stages, from flashing eye patches to yawning and then to bluff charging. Finally, he roared in his ear.

Sphinx never looked at him. Not even when Lothar poked his cheek with a finger. It was as if he really had turned to stone.

Eventually, Lothar was forced to give up and move on. Only

Gerry saw the quick, sidelong glance that Sphinx gave the baboon as he walked away.

Several days after the elephant had sent Gerry flying, the troop stopped again in the shade of a fever tree. They settled down to pick through the grass, repeatedly bringing something to their mouths. As Gerry drew nearer, he could hear the plant grinding between their teeth and he caught the sharp odor of garlic, or something very close to it. He had just started searching for it when Lothar looked up from his feeding and glared at him. Gerry edged behind Zeus so that the leader blocked Lothar's view. But Zeus had his back to him, so Gerry couldn't see what he was eating.

Gerry was startled when Sphinx approached him and plucked a seed pod from the grass at his feet. He watched him strip it between his teeth, extracting the seeds. As he chewed, Sphinx flicked away the pod in a very human gesture and began looking for the next one. The garlic odor rose fresh in Gerry's nostrils. He quickly found a pod and stripped out the seeds as he had seen Sphinx do and bit into one of them. The flavor was more bitter than garlic, but obviously the others considered it food—and good food: they were all eating as fast as they could.

Within a few minutes, unopened pods were hard to find among the seedless husks; the troop had almost plucked the area clean. Gerry looked up. There were still plenty of the pods attached to the branches. He began walking up one of several twisted trunks—against Lothar's protests—and then scampered to a branch that was heavy with the pods. Within seconds, others had joined him. *That's one for the new kid*, thought Gerry.

These pods were juicier and even stronger tasting. They have the experience, thought Gerry, but *you* still have reason.

It was not long before they were all up in the tree, gorging themselves on the seeds. As he pulled the pods from their twigs he noticed that Lothar was working his way up the branch toward him, and he edged away a little. His branch was thinning as he moved, but there was a second branch alongside it, a little higher up, that he was able to hang on to and keep his perch. It also ran behind Lothar's branch, and Gerry saw that, if he moved it, he could poke Lothar with a spike where a branch had been broken off. By pulling on the upper branch, he jabbed Lothar in the small of his back and the monkey whirled with a snarl. Behind him, one of the younger females was feeding. She gave Lothar a quizzical look, as if to ask *what's your problem?* Lothar turned back to gobbling down the seed pods.

Gerry gave him a moment's peace before giving him another jab, and this time Lothar cuffed the female, who retreated, screaming. Gerry couldn't help relishing his small revenge. Lothar stretched to reach a particularly large pod and Gerry jabbed him again, hard, in the bum. Lothar spun around, barking, and the whole troop looked up at him. Gerry wondered if anyone could tell that he was grinning inside, and he got his answer a second later when Lothar turned and came charging up the branch. He retreated as far as he could and dropped to the next branch, just escaping the snap of Lothar's jaws.

Gerry jumped to the grass and scrambled away. What an idiot. Now he'd been driven from one of the richest clusters of pods for the sake of a stupid prank.

Still, it felt good.

He wondered how good it would feel in another few hours when he was hungry again. Even now, he was far from full. He started to move away from the tree, keeping his eyes cast downward to avoid trouble, when a small branch, heavy with seed pods, dropped on the ground in front of him. He lifted his eyes to the tree above him. A baboon sitting next to a freshly broken branch looked away. It was Hector—at least Gerry thought it was Hector. He was still having difficulty telling individual troop members apart, and looking up at him from below wasn't helping. It was definitely a male. Then the baboon turned and Gerry saw Hector's kinked tail.

When the monkey looked down at Gerry again, his expression was unreadable—at least to Gerry. The only time he could read anything from their faces was when they seemed about to attack him. Gerry picked up the branch and looked at it before turning again to Hector. An accident? Maybe. But it didn't look like it would be easy to break off the branch. It was green and healthy and nearly as thick as his arm.

Maybe, just maybe, he had a friend in the troop.

TEMPTATION

Every day, the troop foraged in a circle that began and ended at the sleeping rocks. With the first pale tint of dawn, the baboons left the places where they had huddled alone or in twos or threes, and moved about the rocks, waiting for the sun. When its rays had warmed their bodies, they lowered themselves down the cliff face one ledge at a time. On cooler mornings, they lingered at the base of the monolith before starting out. While the adults dozed and groomed one another, the young raced over the grass in a mad game of tag or swung from the branches of the trees bordering the pond.

During his fifth week of being a baboon, Gerry used this time to gather a pile of stones at the base of the sleeping rocks. Each day, he would add another stone, hoping to keep track of how many days it had been since he was human. He was almost finished arranging the stones when Oscar broke off chasing one of his playmates and took a sudden interest in the pile. Oscar only nursed occasionally now. He was big enough that Mavis spent more time pushing him away from her than feeding him. He watched Gerry add a last stone to the pile, and then he picked it up. Gerry let him handle it for a moment and then pried the stone from the monkey's small hand and put it back in place.

Apparently, in doing so, he created the world's most fascinating rock pile.

Oscar grabbed the stone again, wedged it between his teeth, and tried biting it.

Okay, kid. I know you're looking for a hobby—or maybe just solid food, I don't know—but here's the deal: you see the eight million rocks between here and the horizon? Those are all yours. These thirty right here? These are mine, so—

Oscar took another stone from the pile. By the time Gerry wrested the stone from him, Oscar's squeals of protest were so loud that they brought Mavis, who approached Gerry grunting and smacking her lips as signs of submission. That was as much as she would do to a male—even one of Gerry's low rank.

Lothar had no such reluctance, and apparently he was a friend of the family.

Great.

Gerry could have held on to Oscar. He had seen other males use infants as shields against stronger rivals, but it didn't seem right, somehow. As soon as he released Oscar, who climbed into his mother's arms, Lothar charged in, biting Gerry on the leg as he fled.

Gerry glowered at Lothar from a distance, even though it meant risking another attack. *Fool! You just set back the invention of the baboon calendar who knows how many years.*

Gerry limped around the pond, testing his throbbing leg and brooding over how he might repay Lothar's bullying. He had to make more friends among the other lower-ranking males. Maybe he was Lothar's favorite target right now, but there must have been others before him. All he had to do was find out who they were. No one likes a bully.

He found Chet at the water's edge and tried pointing over and over from the wound on his leg to Lothar. Chet, as always, seemed eager to please, but all he did was stare at Gerry's finger. It dawned on Gerry that baboons didn't really point.

Now that he thought about it, he was sure that he had seen one baboon indicate another by glancing at it, but he had never seen a baboon indicate an inanimate object—apart from Sphinx. He stared at things, but what it meant was a mystery to everyone except Sphinx.

Clearly, organizing a revolt wasn't going to be easy. There was no way to suggest something to another baboon. And yet he knew they formed friendships and alliances. They came to one another's aid in fights. Somehow, he had to make them *want* to help him.

Then Gerry looked up and saw Hector wade out into the grass at the base of the rocks and turn back, waiting for the troop to see him. Usually it was Mavis who started the foraging. He'd watched Hector try to lead the group once before, but no one had followed. As far as Gerry could tell, the troop only followed females to food. It made sense. The females stayed with the troop their whole lives, and eventually learned all the best places to eat within their home range. Today, on some signal invisible to Gerry, one by one the baboons stopped playing or grooming and struck out after Rhona in a ragged line. Hector hung back for a while, pretending not to notice, but before long, he started after them.

As they walked, Gerry noticed that when they passed near tall grass or other cover that could conceal a lion, those at the head of the line would often wait until the rest of the troop caught up. Some of them would form a row and then advance shoulder to shoulder, and the rest would follow behind in a close group.

Maybe it was so that if any one of them was attacked by a predator others could quickly come to his aid. Or maybe, he thought grimly, no one wanted to be at the start or the end of the line in those places. But he also noticed that whatever squabbles arose while they fed or rested disappeared while traveling in open country. There were few enemies they could outrun, here, and nowhere to run to anyway. There was only the troop, and it depended on each of them staying quiet and alert. It was like a fire drill that everyone took very seriously: no shoving, no running, no talking.

They were especially good at the no talking part.

The lead baboon always seemed to have a destination in mind—a place where some food grew in abundance. So it was that each day Gerry learned some new plant—or part of a plant—that he could eat. And yet hunger never left him completely. He kept hoping to find something that would satisfy his appetite. One afternoon he realized that it was not food that he missed but a meal. He had been snacking for over a month now. Five weeks of eating between meals—the kind of thing that would have earned him a slap on the hand from his mother when he was human. But there were no meals here, just a continual effort to satisfy hunger one handful at a time.

Whether or not Rhona had the corn field in mind when she started out that day, Gerry would often wonder. They foraged along the way, but there was little to eat. Every day the dry season wore on, the harder finding food became. Today they dug through the hard ground for corms, but Rhona soon gave up and resumed their march. She seemed to be leading them to a particular place, somewhere beyond the usual circuit that took them to the grove near the river.

They struck out across open grassland, and Gerry passed closer to a herd of giraffes than he had ever been. He could feel the measured thud of their hooves as they strode toward the trees the troop had just left. A tickbird used its sharp claws to climb up one giraffe's neck and stick its head into a twitching ear, looking for parasites. Gerry thought the giraffes were the oddest creatures he had ever seen, with their gearshift horns, huge alien eyes, and long limbs. Their movements reminded him of the cranes he had watched for hours on a construction site back in Croydon. They swung through the troop as if it weren't even there, and then they were gone.

Rhona was headed toward a line of low hills in the distance—or so it seemed to Gerry, who could see nothing between the troop and the horizon. He tried to estimate how far away the hills were, but it wasn't easy. He knew that baboons were very good at seeing things far away. Now he could see so much more detail and at such a distance that it was throwing him off, almost as if he were looking through binoculars. Already he could make out a smudge of brighter green at the base of the hill.

It frustrated him because he had always been good at judging distances. It was a game that he and his father used to play: "How far to those power lines?" Ian would ask as they drove, and then count off the kilometers on the car's odometer.

What would his father be thinking now? He'd be worried, but not as upset as his mother. Gerry imagined her sitting at his bedside in the hospital in Kondoa, adjusting his pillows so they were just so, watching his IV bag to make sure it wasn't empty, reading aloud to him. It comforted him to think of these things.

But then a troubling thought came to Gerry: what if his body wasn't just lying there, as it had been at the crash site? What if he had recovered? Maybe they had gone back to Croydon. Was he watching TV in a living room somewhere? Riding his bike? Already dreading the start of another school year? But a person couldn't be in two places at once, he reasoned. *A person can't be inside a monkey's body, either*, he thought, *but here I am*. So what if there were two Gerrys now? Monkey Gerry, and then human Gerry back home, living his life. No one would even know that anything was wrong. *You're lost and no one's even looking for you.*

A cold swell of panic rolled through him. *You keep thinking that something's wrong, that this is all some mistake that's going to be fixed. But what if this is simply what happens to someone who dies on the savanna? Maybe this is all as natural as rain falling. How would anyone ever know?*

Gerry tried to push the thought from his mind. But the longer he spent in his baboon body, the harder he found it to dispel such ideas.

They walked for nearly an hour. At first, Gerry thought the males were taking positions at the head and tail of the procession so they could better defend the troop. But as the day wore on, it became clear there was no obvious pattern to the group. Gerry walked behind Sphinx, which seemed as safe as anywhere. As always, Chet was behind him.

Hello, I'm Chet. I'll be your shadow for the day. Chet's respectful presentation of his bottom every time he approached Gerry had become as natural as breathing. It was with surprise that Gerry realized he had acquired a sidekick—if not a terribly faithful one. Chet always seemed to disappear whenever Lothar came around.

Gerry could now see that the patch of green was a field of what looked like corn. He could just make out the tall, green stalks standing in rows. Someone had lavished a lot of care on the plants and Hector was leading the troop straight to them. As they drew closer, he could see the shingled roof of a farmhouse on the far side of the field. The corn blocked his view of the rest of the building.

Nearing the barbed-wire fence surrounding the field, the troop became wary, and the baboons glanced around nervously. The fence was designed to keep out grazers like antelope or wildebeest, and didn't present much of a barrier to a monkey. Gerry didn't know if they were just cautious because the corn looked as if it might hide a predator, or if they had been chased off crops before. But once the first baboon had slipped through the wire, the rest followed quickly, spreading among the rows. He hopped onto a fence post and looked around. The raid worried him, but the lure of familiar food was so strong that he soon joined in. Around him, the others began pulling ears from the stalks and stripping away the husks with their nimble hands.

The corn was tasty, if a little hard. It was not the same as he remembered corn, but then he wasn't exactly the same as when he had last tasted it, either.

He quickly stripped the kernels from a cob with his teeth. Looking around at his fellow baboons, he thought they looked oddly human as they held their cobs with both hands and bit into them like hungry picnickers.

They were all so absorbed in feasting that some of them didn't see the young girl ride up on her bicycle from the direction of the farmhouse. She stopped, standing over her rusted Glider, and looked at the baboons. She couldn't have been more than four or five years old. Then she dropped her bike and began throwing rocks at the monkeys. The baboons simply dodged most of them and kept eating. A few of the stones found their marks, but the girl didn't have enough of an arm to do any real damage unless she hit one of them in the face.

Gerry moved a little farther into the leafy tunnel between two rows of plants to avoid being hit, but he feared more for her safety than his own. He wondered what it would take to get one of the others angry enough to attack the kid, and Gerry considered scaring her off. But after a minute or two she seemed to lose interest in the game, pulled the bike back up onto its cracked rubber tires, and pedaled back the way she had come.

They gorged on the corn. The yellow kernels stuck to their fur and lips and soon dozens of cobs littered the ground.

Chet looked at Gerry over his cob. *And how are you enjoying the corn, today? We're finding that this has been a particularly good year for the crop...*

Don't worry, Chet. I won't forget you when it comes time to settle up.

Gerry had just pulled his fourth ear free when a loud crack split the air. The troop scattered, running in panic through the wire fence and back to the open veldt. From his place inside the corn plants, Gerry heard the crack of another gunshot and saw Chet spin and tumble to the ground. Another shot and one of the young females fell.

Gerry moved his head so that he could see beyond the corn leaves. A man dressed in coveralls and a faded shirt steadied a scoped rifle against the corner fence post. Before each shot, he jabbed at his wire-framed glasses with a thick finger, pushing them back into place on the bridge of his nose. His face was shiny with sweat. Each time he fired, another baboon fell, and he cranked another round into the chamber. Gerry tried to scream in warning.

Don't run! Keep down! he wanted to shout. But he was as incapable of shouting as the others were of remaining still. They were a hundred yards away and still the farmer was picking them off.

The whole troop was in flight, but then Zeus, seeing the others fall, stopped and turned back toward their attacker.

The old baboon hesitated only a moment before charging. The farmer took careful aim, leaning into his shot. He couldn't miss with the scoped rifle, and Zeus was still fifty yards away.

Amazed, Gerry watched the farmer lower the rifle from his shoulder and eject an empty clip, then search the pockets of his vest for another. Zeus was too far away to reach him before he reloaded, but Gerry was not. Before he realized what he was doing, Gerry charged out of the corn toward the farmer, barking. The farmer spun toward him, startled. He stumbled backwards, fumbling with the new clip. He palmed it into place and was raising the muzzle to fire again but Gerry already had his hands on the man's jug-handle ears and was sinking his fangs into his shoulder, knocking the astonished farmer over backwards. In the brief time he was on him, before the farmer threw him off, Gerry smelled sweat and soap and toothpaste and a dozen other odors.

The shock on the man's face was nothing compared to his look of horror when he felt Gerry grab the rifle by the shoulder strap and actually pull it over his head. Gerry ran, pulling the rifle away over the grass by the sling.

He glanced back once to see the farmer on his hands and knees, probably searching for his glasses. At first, Gerry scampered away as fast as he could, dragging the rifle, but after a while he turned and slowed. Gradually, he realized he had nothing more to fear from this man. After a moment, Gerry looked down and saw that the farmer's glasses were right there, dangling from the rifle. One of the arms was still caught in the gun's trigger guard.

The farmer sat up and, still breathing hard, squinted at Gerry.

In response, Gerry picked up the glasses and did his best to balance them on his own nose, managing to loop the arms over his ears. He just stood there, staring at the man as intelligently as he could. Then he pushed them back on his snout as he had seen the farmer do.

Now the farmer got to his feet and looked across the open veldt. Without his gun, he was helpless. He stood holding his shoulder with one hand, blood seeping around his fingers, staring at Gerry in open bewilderment. Judging from the thickness of the lenses, Gerry doubted the farmer could see anything at this distance.

Gerry found the rifle's safety and clicked it on. Except for the scope, it was almost identical to his family's gun, an old .303. One of the first things his father had done after setting up the camp for the first time was to show both Gerry and his mother how to use it. He remembered his father's surprise when Joan turned out to be the best shot in the family.

Hearing no more gunshots, some of the troop had turned to see what they were running from. Gerry started toward them, still dragging the rifle.

He first came across young Oscar, whimpering over the body of his mother. Mavis lay crumpled on the grass with her head twisted around. She seemed to be staring at something in the grass in front of her with drying, glassy eyes. Oscar was sitting next to her, trying to push his head under her arm. When he saw Gerry he got up and came over to him, reaching up and clutching at Gerry's hand as if expecting him to do something. Gerry didn't know how to comfort the young baboon.

Chet's body was not far off. Gerry walked over to him and sat there for a moment, looking down at…well, he hadn't exactly been a friend. But he was at least familiar. A familiar nuisance, maybe, but Chet's presence was one of the few things he had been able to cling to since the crash. Looking at him, Gerry suddenly realized what it was he would miss about Chet. As a human being, Gerry's best friend was Milton. Milton might have Gerry's best interests at heart, but he was never short of criticisms, usually wrapped up as advice: "What you need is…" or "You should do this…"

Chet was just there. And maybe that's all a friend was. Someone who was there.

And then Lothar came toward him, eye patches flashing. He sat down heavily and yawned, exposing his enormous teeth—a clear signal for Gerry to move on. But Gerry did not get up. Instead he dragged the rifle closer. He lifted the barrel in one hand and with the other he slipped off the safety.

Lothar turned his head toward him, yawning and making strangled barking sounds, growing more agitated. In another few seconds he would charge. Gerry angled the barrel at Lothar's chest and slipped a finger inside the trigger guard. A twitch of his finger could make life much easier and send a swaggering bully from the world. It would be over, Gerry reasoned, without Lothar ever knowing what had happened. He would not have to suffer. This was infinitely preferable to whatever death awaited him on the veldt one day.

He felt the trigger pulling back against the crook of his finger.

But he couldn't do it—even thought he knew that no one would ever know what he had done. He just knew it was wrong.

When it came down to it, he couldn't imagine standing before his parents and telling them he had shot an animal. Especially a baboon.

It would be unfair. And not just because killing him was a punishment out of proportion to the injuries he had suffered at Lothar's teeth and claws. It was the gun. Using it to kill would be wrong. But he would not suffer the old tyrant, who was still yawning and flashing his eyepatches, warming up to his attack.

He gripped the rifle, preparing himself.

When Lothar finally charged, Gerry pointed the muzzle away and squeezed the trigger. The crack of the gunshot at point-blank range was deafening.

Lothar spun and ran, followed by the rest of the troop. When Gerry looked, he saw the farmer sprinting for all he was worth in the opposite direction, making for the shelter of his corn field.

Gerry left the glasses where the man would find them, on one of the fenceposts.

THE BABOON CLUB

Something had changed. Their eyes held his a second longer before flicking away. They gave him an inch more space as they shouldered past him—or maybe it was an inch less. Gerry didn't know what it was, but the troop's attitude toward him shifted after he attacked the farmer.

That evening, as they prepared to scale the sleeping rocks, Oscar crawled into Gerry's lap and began grooming him. Young baboons often sought the friendship of new adult males who had joined the troop—not that they had any way of knowing that Gerry was new. He must have smelled and looked as he always had. It felt strange, at first, to have this little being picking through his fur. As a human, Gerry could barely sit still for a haircut, but he could not turn him away. Fellow orphans, thought Gerry. He tried not to squirm.

As night fell, and after the others had climbed the cliffs, Gerry found a hiding place for the rifle. He crept into the trees at the base of the rocks—a place he would never have ventured after dark, ordinarily, but the weight of the rifle in his hands made him bold. He hid it inside the hollow of an enormous baobab tree. It was too heavy to carry from place to place, and when the rains came it would be ruined. But until then he would have the option of using it—if things got really bad.

Dragging the gun all the way home and to its hiding place had been exhausting. By the time he climbed the warm rocks to the summit, he was almost asleep on his feet. For the first time, he took a place up higher, among the others—even if it was at the margins of the troop. As he lay down, he saw Sphinx walk to the edge of the cliff and stand looking out over the veldt. He was still there, watching the stars pierce the darkness, when Gerry fell asleep.

In the morning, he awoke to a fresh sorrow. He took a moment to study the others sleeping around him and did a quick count. There were at least four adults missing, including Mavis. As the others roused themselves, Gerry wondered what they were thinking. Some of them would wake up to find themselves without a sister, a brother, or an aunt they had known their whole lives. He tried to see if there was any difference in the way they sat up and looked around. What did a sad baboon look like? It was impossible to tell if they felt their losses and just carried on anyway, or if they just forgot.

But Oscar had not forgotten. This morning, he went to the edge of the cliff and called out over the veldt, again and again, a small bleating cry.

Gerry resolved to return to the site of the plane crash. The rifle he had taken from the farmer might not be a practical weapon, but it had taught him something: he had advantages, and he could use them to make his life easier and, if he were careful, longer. He let the others get ahead of him and then looked around, hoping to find the way back to the plane.

He knew that baboons had a strong sense of direction, and could return to almost any place they chose, but he couldn't remember the way. He tried to recall where the sun had been in the sky as he traveled. He tried to remember some of the landmarks he had seen along the way, but his memories of the trip were a jumble.

Somehow he was going about this the wrong way. Reason was only confusing him. He sat down in the grass and tried to clear his mind of everything but the plane. He turned and faced in the opposite direction and again pictured the downed plane.

When he felt he was facing the right direction, he started walking—slowly at first, and then with growing confidence. With each step, the certainty that he was heading toward the plane grew. It was still dangerous to travel without the troop, but at least now he knew how to feed himself. He kept walking, and late in the afternoon he saw the jut of the plane's tail on the horizon.

Before he even entered the cockpit, he knew that Stan's body had been removed. Gerry was learning to trust his nose. He dragged open the door and stepped into the darkened cabin.

A lizard scurried away in the dark. He smelled blood and cut steel. He smelled the vinyl of the pilot's chair, and something else soaked into it: sweat. It took him a moment to realize that this was the scent of a human being.

It was a relief that someone had taken Stan away. Maybe Gerry hadn't liked him much but he deserved better than to have his bones scattered and gnawed upon by hyenas.

Some of the plane's flight instruments had also been removed, leaving holes in the instrument panel with wires and connectors creeping out of them like vines. Gerry searched the cockpit, not sure of what he was looking for. Finding nothing of use, he went back into the main passenger cab and looked around.

In the end, he settled on a roll of packing tape. He had hoped to find the tool chest but it, too, had been taken. Everything else he wanted to take, from makeshift canteens to knives, was too heavy. But he already had at least one use for the packing tape in mind.

It was on the way back, not far from the plane, that he found Stan's foot. He knew that it was Stan's because it was still in its running shoe, and Gerry recognized it. Ants swarmed over it. Two other bones, long enough that they could only have been from a leg, rested nearby. There was no other clothing anywhere. Gerry reasoned that they had returned for the body, but not before some scavenger had gnawed off the leg and dragged it from the plane. It angered Gerry to find it like this. Maybe they had come back for Stan, but they had been too late to get all of him. And how hard could they have looked? The leg was right here.

He took the longest of the bones with him. There was no way for him to bury it, but perhaps Stan could still have a kind of revenge on the veldt that had hammered the life from him.

He started out again, knowing that he would not make it back to the troop before dark. He had traveled for just over an hour when he reached a lone acacia tree. After his encounter with the leopard, he knew how important it was to be able to move from the outer branches of one tree to those of another, something a leopard could not do. But he did not see any stands of trees that he could reach before dark. He decided to stay here and climbed as high as he could into the tree's branches.

What little sleep he had was filled with dreams. He kept having one about trying to pull on a coat. Even in his dreams, he was a baboon. His thin arms kept churning in the heavy fabric, searching vainly for a sleeve hole. He had a lot of dreams about clothing and dressing, but always in his monkey's body.

At first light he awoke in the crotch of a branch, with his arm through the roll of packing tape he had taken from the plane. Stan's leg bone had fallen to the ground, and he climbed down to retrieve it. But first he took a good look around.

The grass was wet with dew, and he shivered in the cold morning air.

He started walking to warm himself. It wasn't easy, trying to walk while hanging onto both the bone and the roll of tape. After a while, he peeled off a length of tape and stuck them both to the fur on his upper arm. It was uncomfortable, but it worked. As he walked, he searched for a suitable stone from which to make his weapon, but the soil here was nearly free of rocks. Isn't this where the first tools were made? Africa? It was a miracle the stone age had ever gotten off the ground with pickings like this.

He had walked for perhaps a mile when he found what he was looking for: a stone the size and shape of a human heart. He braced himself, and then ripped off the tape stuck to his arm in one quick motion.

He held the stone against the head of the leg bone and began wrapping the packing tape around them. He had to use enough tape to bind the rock securely to the bone, but he didn't want to pad it too much. His hands just weren't as nimble or as strong as his old, human hands, but after a while he had what looked like a pretty good tomahawk.

No scissors. He bit off the end of the tape and examined his cudgel. He beat the ground with the stone end a few times and felt the weight of it in his hand. It was easier to swing, he found, if he grasped the handle about halfway up its length.

But it was impossible to carry. What he needed was a shoulder sling. More tape. He stuck the sticky sides of two pieces together to form a strip a little longer than the cudgel, then taped it to either end of the handle. It made a pretty good shoulder strap, except that he didn't have much in the way of shoulders and the plastic tape was too slippery. A folded piece of tape in the middle of the strap, sticky side out, solved that problem.

The curious thing was that when he made it back to the troop that night, no one seemed to take the slightest notice of the weapon. Gerry didn't know what he had expected. He thought he might have at least drawn a few stares but it just didn't seem to register. It was as if clubs had gone out of style and they were all too embarrassed to mention it.

He stashed the roll of tape with the rifle.

That night, before he climbed to his place in the sleeping rocks, he stopped to count the stones in his pile and a curious thing happened. He tried to count the pile three times, but every time he reached twenty-three, he had to stop. He could not remember, for the life of him, what came after twenty-three. He could see that there were roughly as many stones remaining in the pile as he had counted. So he knew that he had counted half of them. He knew that if he multiplied twenty-three by two, he would get forty-six. He had been a baboon for roughly forty-six days, give or take a stone or two.

He could do the math, but he couldn't count past twenty-three, and that was troubling to Gerry. He tried for an hour. He counted until his head throbbed, and the darkness fell around him. He would have given anything for a pen and paper. He wanted to write down what had happened. Had he never been able to count past twenty-three since being a monkey or had he lost his ability to count sometime in the last forty-six days?

Far into the night, long after he had climbed the rocks and taken his place among the slow-breathing bodies of the troop, Gerry was still counting to himself.

THE KILL

It was Sphinx who first noticed the gazelles. They were nearly home, returning to the sleeping rocks after a day's foraging. The rest of the troop had stopped to pick berries from a clump of needle bushes when Gerry looked up and saw Sphinx in the classic Sphinx pose, gazing at a small herd of Thompsons not far away. They were playing some kind of game, charging and chasing one another. There was something both graceful and toy-like in the gazelles' tightly sprung movements and Gerry found it almost hypnotic. In the twilight, he could see the ripple of every muscle beneath their short coats. One by one, other members of the troop took an interest in Sphinx, and then what he was watching. After a while, Gerry realized that it was only the other males who were looking. The females continued to graze.

Then Sphinx got to his feet and started walking in the direction of the gazelles. As if in some silent agreement, the male baboons followed him, and Gerry had the feeling that this was something they had done before. He also had the impression that he was expected to take part, and he was suddenly uneasy.

So were the gazelles, who immediately noticed the change in the troop's attitude. They stopped their play and turned their attention to the baboons. Gerry was certain that at any second they would run. Once they did, it would all be over. They didn't have a hope of catching the gazelles once they had bolted.

When the tommies ran, Gerry noticed one loop back toward them before bounding away a short distance and then stopping. It was almost as if it was taunting the troop. *Come on!* it seemed to say. *Just try to catch me!*

But Sphinx's eyes were no longer on the gazelle. He was searching a clump of tall grass not far from where they had been grazing. He took a few steps toward it and, again, the gazelle paraded in front of the troop.

But Sphinx was not to be deterred. At once, he and Lothar bolted toward the tall grass and pounced upon a fawn hiding there. It kicked and twisted, but Lothar had it by the forelegs and Sphinx the hind. There was a brief tug of war that ended with Lothar biting Sphinx, who screamed and ran off, his tail in the air. Lothar wrapped the prize in his arms, trying to contain the kicking gazelle. It didn't make a sound, but the mother stood nearby and charged Lothar once, who dragged the writing fawn in Gerry's direction. The rest of the males in the troop followed, hoping for some portion of the kill.

Lothar raised the fawn, still clamped in the crooks of his arms, and bit into the belly. The fawn screamed and Lothar tore out a length of intestine.

Horrified, Gerry watched as Lothar bit again and again into the still-living fawn. Gerry knew that baboons did not deliver a killing bite the way cats did. Either they didn't care or didn't know how. But Gerry couldn't stand it. He slipped the sling of the cudgel over his head and strode toward Lothar. Gerry brought the head of his club down on the fawn's skull, ending its glimpse of a life.

Lothar leapt back, dropping the dead fawn. For a moment, everyone just looked at him, too startled to move. But in the instant before Lothar charged, Gerry saw his expression flash from amazement to rage. Gerry drew back the cudgel as he retreated and struck at Lothar as he rushed toward him, catching him just behind the brow ridge with the club's stone heart. Lothar collapsed, twitching, to the grass.

The others looked at Gerry, unsure of what they had just seen or what they should do next. They wanted the fawn but their opportunity to take it had somehow ended.

They were confused. It had begun as a fight, but then…it was simply over. And now Gerry just stood there, one hand on the cudgel, staring at Lothar's lifeless body. The others looked from Gerry to the fawn. Clearly, Gerry was somehow the victor. No one made a move toward the kill.

Gerry didn't want it either. But he knew he was expected to claim his prize. He glanced down at the fawn. Mercifully, it had stopped moving. Trembling, he grabbed it by the leg and pulled it closer. The others continued to watch him as he drew back a step, clutching the body.

The mother gazelle paced nearby. She was clearly upset, but unwilling to approach her dead fawn.

And what happened next Gerry could hardly believe. The smell of the fawn's blood, warm and metallic, rose in his nostrils and suddenly Gerry's muzzle was in its belly, feasting on the steaming jumble of meat and organs.

He had eaten nothing but morsels of insects and roots and seeds for more than a month and here was food he could devour. It was a meal. He had never tasted anything so good in his life. Only the need for air caused him to withdraw his snout, gasping.

He retreated from the other baboons, but by now even those who had not joined the hunting party gathered nearby. He shared only with Oscar, who came begging.

When he had had his fill, Gerry dropped what was left of the carcass, and the others fell upon it in a grotesque tug of war. Soon only the head and hooves dangled from the stretched hide, which was rasped clean of all else. A female crunched on a bone. It was Zeus who finally cracked the skull in his enormous jaws and consumed the brain.

No one showed any interest in the cudgel, the trigger of it all. Gerry picked it up where it had fallen and worked the sling over his shoulder. It was only after the gazelle's remains had passed through every hand in the troop that a few turned their attention to Lothar, who was sprawled upon the grass. Zeus came over and stared first at the body, then at Gerry, with indifference or approval, he could not tell. But then he approached Gerry, something he had never done before. Gerry was careful to avoid the old baboon's eyes, and looked off toward the horizon as Zeus fingered the cudgel. For a time, he seemed to study the same, distant spot where Gerry had fixed his gaze. It was as if he realized, somehow, that the cudgel was the key to what had taken place, even if he could not understand how. Then Zeus moved off and the rest of the troop followed.

For the rest of the day, their behavior toward Gerry was the same as it had always been. But that evening, as they settled in at the base of the sleeping rocks, Oscar again approached Gerry and began to groom him. Gerry was getting used to the grooming and had seen the effect it had on the others. It was like a drug to them, and the more hands doing the grooming, the more powerful it was.

Soon Oscar was joined by one of his playmates, who also began picking and sweeping through the fur on Gerry's body, and he found himself beginning to drowse. He caught himself fighting to stay awake. Why he struggled, he didn't know. He was as safe here as anywhere. The troop would be watching for predators, and nothing could happen to him with two of the infants so near. Especially, he thought to himself with satisfaction bruised by guilt, with Lothar gone.

When Gerry awoke, he was alone and it was dark. The rest of the troop had climbed the sleeping rocks. He peered out into the darkness. Without a moon, he could see very little.

A firefly scratched the darkness in front of him, blinked, and spiraled away.

Gerry realized that he had been awoken by something.

The crickets had stopped, and in the silence he heard a twig snap. Something was moving in the grove off to his right, a blotch of deeper black.

Gerry did not wait to learn what it was. He turned and began climbing the rock face. Only when he had reached a safe height did he turn and scan the dark below him.

A warm wind rose along the stone face, lifting the fur of his cape. Still he saw nothing. But he was certain that something down there waited for him. In a brief panic, he felt for the cudgel. It was still there, head down, strapped across his back.

Gerry climbed higher, and a few moments later he was at the summit. There, he could just make out the dark humps of the troop against the starry sky. As he took his place among them, he realized that the sight had become a comfort to him.

What he really wanted, at that moment, was to sit in front of a fire and warm himself for just a little while. Without the drowsing effect of Oscar's grooming, he didn't want to close his eyes. And when he finally did, he saw his own small hand grasping the club as it struck Lothar's skull. Over and over, he heard the terrible crunch of rock meeting bone. The worst part of it was that the club's stone head just stayed where it had connected until Gerry pulled it away.

Only a few days ago, he had been unable to shoot Lothar with the rifle. He remembered clearly deciding that it would have been wrong. But today he had killed him without hesitation.

How could that be?

As he squirmed and turned, trying to find the right hollow in the rock, the same absurd answer kept coming to him: he had taken the gun, but the club he had made with his own hands.

BATTLE OF THE BOBCAT

The next morning, the troop acted as if nothing had happened. Gerry had expected some kind of mood change. With Lothar, the troop's top bully, removed, Gerry had thought maybe everyone would just get along. Or at least leave each other alone.

But Gerry noticed little difference in the baboons' behavior. There were the usual squabbles. A number of males were pestering Lucinda, a female who had become receptive to mating. Hector was among them, doing his best, but she seemed to have no interest in entertaining a male of his low rank.

Gerry felt more relaxed himself without having to worry about where Lothar was and whether he might be doing something to provoke him.

Zeus led the troop that day, but it didn't seem to be to anywhere in particular. His foraging seemed somewhat aimless. They found some seed pods in the morning, but not enough to satisfy anyone. They were moving across the open veldt, the kind of travel that made everyone nervous. Gerry was annoyed because he doubted that whatever riches they came across would be worth the risk.

But within half an hour they came to a termite mound. The troop would have simply passed by, but Sphinx crouched in front of the tower and began one of his staring matches. It never hurt, Gerry had learned, to pay attention to whatever Sphinx was paying attention to, and he paused to look at the mound. After a moment, Hector walked over and worked at tearing it open. Gerry tried to help him but the weird, gray spires felt as strong as concrete to his hands.

Then Gerry got an idea and swung at it with his cudgel. He knocked off a chunk of the tower, exposing the dank interior. Soldiers swarmed out of the wreckage to defend the colony with their enormous jaws, and the troop gathered around to feast.

The trick, as Gerry learned from watching the others, was to work quickly: get them into your mouth and crush them between your molars before they could bite you too many times with their pincers. Gerry was also using a stem of grass, which he fed into the writhing mass of bodies. On the way to his mouth, the angry insects concentrated their attack on the stem. He used his teeth to strip them off.

Back in Croydon, he'd seen a chimpanzee use a similar trick on a nature documentary. Around him, the others were still using their hands. *Obviously not getting the Discovery Channel*, thought Gerry.

It didn't take long for the workers to seal up their nest again with something they vomited from their tiny mouths, but it took only a few seconds for Gerry to open it again with his club. The troop fed until they were satisfied—or at least their mouths were too sore from bites to eat any more. One by one, they moved off in search of a more agreeable meal. *Termites*. Gerry thought. *The snack that bites back.*

By MID-AFTERNOON, Gerry found that he was more thirsty than hungry, and he hoped that Zeus was leading them to water. He was grateful when they stopped in a grove of umbrella trees. Gerry leaned against the trunk of one of the trees and watched the troop.

A dry stream bed ran through the grove. After a few minutes, Lucinda walked out to the center of the dried-up watercourse and sniffed at a depression in the sand, where someone or something had been digging. She stared at it, as if expecting something to emerge from the ground. Then she began pawing at the sand, and finally digging in earnest. Soon she had excavated a narrow hole as deep as her elbow. She carefully pulled out one handful of sand after another. After a few minutes she was rewarded with a patch of moist sand, and in another moment a dirty pool collected at the bottom of the pocket. The hole was just big enough for Lucinda to insert her muzzle, and Gerry heard her slurping at the pool.

She had taken only a few sips when one of the males who had been following her for most of the afternoon nudged her aside. He stuck his snout into the hole and began drinking. *That might get you a drink, but nothing else*, thought Gerry.

While he was drinking, Lucinda walked over to Hector and presented to him. But it wasn't the casual gesture of respect that presenting to a higher-ranking baboon meant. She stuck her rump high into the air and held it there. It was the female baboon's invitation to mate.

It was what Hector had been waiting for, but at that moment the other male sat up and saw Lucinda presenting to Hector. He charged at them, barking. Lucinda ran in one direction and Hector the other. The male chased Lucinda and quickly caught up, biting her on the back while she squealed in pain and fear. When he was done punishing her, he turned back to Hector, who stood next to Gerry.

The male was bigger than either of them, but he hesitated when he saw Hector and Gerry standing side by side. Hector stamped the ground with his front paw, took a step toward the male, then turned back to Gerry. Then he did it again. Gerry knew exactly what Hector was asking. *Come on, we can take him!* he was saying.

Hector charged toward the male, and had covered half the distance between them when he glanced back and saw that Gerry hadn't moved. At the last second, he veered off and the male, more than a match for either of them alone, chased him up one of the acacia trees. With some relief, Gerry saw that that seemed to be enough for the male, who was far more angry at Lucinda.

Gerry walked over to the tree and looked up at Hector. He felt bad for his friend, and more than a little guilty. All the same, he had no intention of risking being attacked and bitten just because Hector wanted to mate with some female. The male probably wouldn't have done serious damage to Gerry in a fight, but he knew that even minor bite wounds sometimes became infected. His parents had seen baboons die from such wounds.

Hector was clearly angry with him. He wouldn't leave the tree where he had taken refuge until the rest of the troop resumed foraging. Even after he climbed down, he refused to go near Gerry for the rest of the afternoon.

As they followed Zeus farther out onto the veldt, Gerry thought more and more about his failure to help Hector. It wasn't just his own cowardice that he regretted but, as the day wore on, he realized that he had missed an opportunity. Maybe being bitten by Lucinda's suitor was taking a chance, but how much more likely was he to be bitten if he stayed at the bottom of the troop's pecking order? Killing Lothar might have increased his rank in the troop, but it wouldn't last for long if he didn't do something to hold onto his improved position. He would need help for that, and Hector had been a friend.

It was a stupid mistake. Gerry vowed to himself that he would not repeat it.

They had been walking for just about an hour when Gerry spotted something orange against the yellow veldt, just below the horizon. As they drew closer, he saw what appeared to be a cage of painted metal sticking above the grass. At first Gerry thought it must be some kind of animal trap. He had no idea what it would be doing out here in the middle of the veldt, far from the nearest farm or building. It was as if it had just fallen out of the sky.

It took Gerry a few minutes to realize that that was exactly where it had come from.

It was the machine he and his father had pushed from the Skyvan when they were trying to keep the plane in the air. He was looking at the cab of the front-end loader, sticking above the grass. By chance, the Bobcat had landed upright, but all four of its balloon tires had burst on impact and it was buried up to its axles in the hard ground. Other than that, it was surprisingly intact. It looked much as it had in the airplane—its orange paint as bright as if it had just left the factory.

Then Gerry saw that Sphinx was staring at it. Sphinx always took his staring matches seriously, but this one was different. Something about the machine had upset Sphinx. Instead of crouching in his usual pose, he was pacing back and forth, growling, while keeping his eyes fixed on the front-end loader. Maybe it was the machine's headlights, which looked a little like eyes.

To calm him down, Gerry climbed into the cab—more of a jungle gym than a true cab—but this only upset Sphinx more. While the whole troop looked on, Gerry worked the levers controlling the machine's drive wheels.

Hector climbed into the bucket and, after a moment, Oscar joined him. The others gathered around to see what they were doing. Suddenly, Sphinx charged the machine. He jumped from the wheel onto the hydraulic arm and bit the rubber hose that fed it.

Then Gerry saw that the key was still in the ignition.

He turned it. It produced only a clicking sound, but when he pressed a button on the instrument panel the horn sounded, shrill in the quiet of the savanna. Several of the baboons who had perched on the machine scattered, but when they turned and saw Gerry still sitting in the driver's seat, they drifted back to the Bobcat and climbed back onto it.

A few of them were gnawing on the tires, and Sphinx tried his teeth on one of the hoses once again. This time, he punctured the rubber and a jet of fluid erupted from the hose.

He scampered away, barking and shaking his head, but soon circled back again. He scaled the machine and thumped the roll cage with his fist. Zeus also climbed onto the top of the cage and bounced against the cab, pounding it with his feet. Hector roared from the bucket. Oscar chattered and ran in circles around them. The whole troop was screaming and barking while Gerry honked the horn again and again and yanked on the levers. He yelled and barked as the troop worked itself into frenzy against the imagined enemy.

As they pulled and pushed and jumped on the machine Gerry looked up from his place in the cab and caught a glint of light halfway to the horizon.

In the distance, he saw the distinct roofline of a second and much more familiar machine rising above the grass. It was a Land Rover. He would never have been able to make out with his human eyes what he was seeing now: someone was watching him through the open passenger window, using a pair of binoculars. The person lowered the binoculars, so she might believe what she was seeing with her own eyes.

It was Gerry's mother.

Gerry watched Joan raise the binoculars to her face, and he tried to imagine her view of the troop. After a moment, his father got out and walked around to her side of the truck. She handed him the binoculars. Even at this distance, Gerry knew they would recognize the baboons they had studied for so long. They were far enough away that the rest of the troop took no notice of them. After their long absence, his parents would know that they had to approach the troop over a period of days if they were not to alarm them.

With a curious dread, Gerry waited to see if a third person got out of the truck. He half expected to see himself push open the back door and step out to stretch his legs. Had that happened, he knew that there would be no way back. It would be even worse than hearing that his human body had died. But there appeared to be no one else in the truck. After ten minutes of trading the binoculars and watching the troop, they got back into the truck and drove off. Gerry watched the Land Rover drag a wake of dust into the distance and then it was gone. He knew that he would have to follow it. Leaving the other baboons to their battle with the Bobcat, he started walking in the direction his parents had taken.

THE WAY BACK

The heat of the day brought a complete quiet. Even the flies retreated to wherever it was they went when it became too hot.

As Gerry walked, he felt the blaze of the sun on his back. He remembered hearing someone—maybe his father—talking about a theory that, millions of years ago, right here on the savanna, the ancestors of human beings had started walking upright not just to free their hands, but to cool their bodies. By standing up, they raised their bodies a little higher off the ground where there was a bit of a breeze. And five million years after that, they invented the hat.

We're on a roll, thought Gerry. We just keep getting cooler and cooler.

He thought about the baboon council and wondered again if they were responsible for his metamorphosis. If so, why had they made him a baboon and not some other animal? Maybe they had had no choice. Maybe there was a zebra council and an elephant council for the other conversions. Or maybe he had just dreamed the whole thing and there was no baboon council.

He realized that this was the first opportunity he'd had since joining the troop to just think. He used to spend a lot of time just thinking when he was a person. But being a baboon was exhausting. Somebody was always at you: picking through your fur, shoving you away from your food, asking you to help fight their battles. You never had a moment to yourself. It was worse than being at school.

It struck him, then, how much they were the same—being a baboon and being in school. In either case, he just wanted to be left alone.

Once, after he'd come back to Croydon halfway through the school year, they sent him to see the school psychologist—to make sure he was "getting along," that he was "adjusting." He sat down in front of Mr. Allen. Mr. Allen was a fat man, under pressure from everything he wore. The waistband of his pants. The bracelet of his watch. The arms of his glasses. They all seemed to cut into his fleshy body.

"And how are things going?" he had asked Gerry. "Settling in all right?"

Why don't you wear something that fits you? Gerry had wanted to ask him. *Because you're thinking you're going to lose that weight, aren't you Mr. Allen? You're thinking no, no this is just a temporary condition. I'm going to lay off the chips and take up jogging. Buying a watch band that isn't stretched to the breaking point would just be resigning myself to being fat.*

But you are fat, Mr. Allen. And you're going to be fat for the rest of your life.

And you're going to be a baboon, Gerry. Not a particularly good one, I might add, if you don't pull up these grades.

Gerry looked around the veldt and tried to remember the last time he had thought of his appointment with Mr. Allen. He might never have thought of him again, but here he was surrounded by grass with the African sun like a hot brand on his back, and he was thinking of someone he'd met only once more than two years ago.

He wished the baboon council had made him into something simpler. Maybe a giraffe. Just eat grass and admire the view every time you raised your head. Think of the view.

SOMETIME AROUND SUNSET, he reached the twin ruts of the Land Rover's tracks. At first he feared he would have trouble following them in the dark. But there was a faint odor of burnt grass where the stalks had brushed against the belly of the truck's engine. Beneath that, Gerry could detect the smells of motor oil and rubber. He did not have to wander far from the tracks before his nose brought him back on course. As he traveled, the odors grew stronger. Within an hour, he was certain that he was catching up.

Gerry felt for the cudgel on his back. Alone and traveling at night over the open grassland, it felt good to have it near. Once, a pack of hyenas passed close to him. Luckily, they were upwind, and Gerry detected their musky scent before they found his. He held his breath while they crossed the Land Rover's track in the darkness behind him. If they had smelled him, apparently they did not deem a lone baboon worth pursuing. There were easier meals on the veldt at night.

The walk gave him time to consider what he would do when he caught up to his parents. What would he say to them?

Say to them? *You're a baboon for God's sake. You can't "say" anything.*

All right. Poor choice of words. But even if he could speak, what could he say?

Was there even any point in trying to tell them what had happened? His parents knew no more about fourteen-year-old boys turning into baboons than he did. He had no reason to believe they were going to have any brilliant insights into fixing the problem.

He just wanted to know what had happened to his human body. And that his parents were all right.

That wasn't quite true. More than anything, he just wanted to be with them.

He had been walking for just over an hour when he followed the tracks over a low ridge and out of the dark distance a familiar sight rose: two canvas tents, one of them lit from within by a Coleman lantern. For a moment, he couldn't be certain that it was his parents' encampment, and not someone else's.

Then the wind shifted direction, carrying on it a delicious aroma. It was his father's barbecued chicken, and the odor was as irresistible to him as it was familiar. He started down the gentle slope toward the cooking tent.

He approached quietly, away from the door. He could hear the clinking and ringing of the dinner dishes being washed and dried, and for a time, the sound was comforting to him. But as it went on, he was disturbed by what he didn't hear. There was only silence between them, and that was unusual for his parents at mealtime. Sometimes they argued. Sometimes they just described little things they had each seen the baboons doing: Sphinx had become obsessed with a particular rock; Oscar was stung by a bee. Most nights, Gerry could hardly get a word in edgewise. Now, there were only the sounds of cleaning up. He sat listening for a long time, but the silence only deepened with the night.

His mother finally spoke: "I'm going back tomorrow."

"What...? To Kondoa? We just got here."

"I know. I just...I keep thinking of him waking up in that hospital room and no one being there."

"We said we'd give it at least a week. Come on now. I want us to spend at least a few days in the field."

"I didn't say you had to come back, too," said his mother.

"Well how am I going to get to the troop if you take the truck?"

"I could fly."

"Joan, the grant money's almost gone. We can't afford any more charters!"

"But what if he wakes up?"

"You heard the doctors. The chances of him regaining consciousness—"

"What if he did? What if he only woke up for a minute before..."

His father tried to be as gentle with her as he could. "All I was going to say is that the chances of him waking up and us actually being there are very slight unless we practically live at the hospital."

"But at least we could be there within the hour. It'll take us half a day to get back from here."

"The hospital said they'd radio the ranger station if there was any change."

"It's not the same."

Then, for a long time, no one said anything. In the silence, Gerry could almost feel his father give in.

"All right," he said quietly. "If it's still too soon for you, it's too soon."

"*He's not dead!*"

Soon Gerry's father came out of the cook tent and began to collect firewood from around the camp. He piled it away from the tent and searched his pockets. He went back into the kitchen and Gerry heard the familiar sound of him rummaging through one of the big, aluminum lockboxes where they kept their food safe from animals. He returned a moment later with a box of matches.

Building a fire was what Gerry's father did whenever he was troubled or had something to mull over. His grandmother once told Gerry, with obvious pride, "That boy could start a fire with nothing more than a couple of wet dogs and a bowl of oatmeal." A clear picture rose in Gerry's mind, a memory from the day his father had shown him how to make a fire.

He saw him on his knees, blowing a flame to life beneath a teepee of dried grass and tinder, just as he was doing now. He fed sticks into the fire, one by one. "Just enough to keep it going," he told Gerry. Firewood was not to be wasted—especially here, where trees were precious.

Now he saw flames leap from the pyramid of tinder, and his father stood back. The light from the fire grew brighter and when his father looked up again from the flames, he saw Gerry in the orange light.

Gerry sat back on his haunches, so that he was in a squatting position. He hoped that it would reassure his father.

Ian Copeland peered at his son and took a step forward. Gerry stood up again and his father stopped. He didn't know why, but Gerry didn't want him to come any closer. Then, without thinking, Gerry slipped a paw underneath the strap he had made for the cudgel and adjusted it slightly.

That got his attention.

"Joan...?"

From inside the sleeping tent: "What is it?"

When his father didn't answer, she came out of the tent and just stood there, looking from her husband to the fire, which was dying down.

"What is it?" she asked again.

Ian put a finger to his lips and pointed into the darkness. Then he returned to the fire and threw on a few sticks, building the flames again. After a moment, Gerry could tell that she could also see him.

"What is that he's...wearing?"

Gerry's father shook his head, baffled. "It must be a pet."

"Out here…?"

"Well, whatever it is, someone must have put it on him," said his father. "He didn't make it himself."

Wanna bet?

"You know," said Ian, "I could swear…"

"What?"

"I could swear it's the same one that was hanging around the crash."

"Are you sure?"

"Not really. Probably not. Look, it must be a pet that someone let go. Otherwise, why would it be hanging around? It's looking for a handout."

"He does look awfully thin."

"And that thing he's wearing over his shoulder…it almost looks like a club."

Joan stepped forward and peered at Gerry's cudgel. "Is that a bone?"

"It looks like it."

"I don't like it hanging around here," said his mother.

Ian frowned. "Why not?"

"I don't know. It just bothers me."

After a minute of staring at Gerry, Joan declared that she was going to bed.

"I'll be in in a little while," said Ian.

They sat, separated by fire, for a long time. Gerry imagined what he would say if he could speak. As the night air grew colder, he edged closer to the flames. The heat on his face and belly felt good. He watched his father sink into his chair.

They had been sitting for half an hour and the fire was dying down. Without thinking, Gerry picked up a stick and tossed it onto the embers.

For a moment, Gerry thought his father hadn't noticed. But then he moved his hand from his chin to his knee, and looked at him with a mixture of fascination and disbelief.

"Who are you?" his father asked.

Gerry wanted to answer him. He thought he might be able to prove to him who he was. The hardest part was getting his father to believe he was something other than just a baboon, and he seemed ready for that. It was just a feeling he had. Gerry could go to the tent, find some object that had been his. Or a photograph. He knew there were pictures of him with his parents. Point to his father, point to the father in the picture. Point to Joan, point to his mother in the picture. Point to himself, point to Gerry in the picture. He could make them understand. But could he make them believe?

He knew his father. He was intelligent. He was flexible in his thinking. His mother...that would be harder.

And if he convinced them of who he was, what then? What could they do about it? They couldn't change Gerry back into a boy. He didn't know how this had happened, but it was clearly beyond his power, or any other human being's, to change it.

So even if they did, somehow, accept the truth, as strange as it was, what would they all do? Would Gerry live as their pet? Continue in home schooling? He could eat sandwiches and fruit and cooked meat. He could even do chores around camp. Help out. They'd make a hell of a team. He and his parents would be the foremost experts on baboon behavior in the world. Hands down.

And then something occurred to Gerry, something that frightened him far more than anything that had happened to him so far. Even if they all could come to such an arrangement, even if it comforted or pleased his mother, could he live that way?

Gerry adjusted the strap on his cudgel, turned away from the fire, and started off into darkness. He looked behind him, and saw his father on his feet.

He heard his name, a sound he had longed for more than anything else in the days since he had changed.

Then again.

It was all that Gerry could do to keep going.

MOVING ON

Gerry didn't make it far before he decided that he owed his parents some kind of explanation. That was the wrong word; he could hardly explain what had happened to him. But a farewell of some kind was in order, even if he could not face his parents directly.

When he was far enough away, he looked back at his father standing at the edge of that trembling puddle of light in the dark.

Could he really do this? He believed he could survive as a baboon. He could find food and defend his place in the troop. But what would that mean if he never said another word, saw someone smile for him, or heard his name spoken? How long could he play the memories of these things in his mind before they lost all meaning? Already, he was an echo of his life, growing fainter with each reverberation. When even that was gone, nothing could bring him back.

All he was doing was haunting himself.

And if he were some kind of ghost, shouldn't he be moving on? Isn't that what ghosts did when they eventually figured it out, or forgave themselves, or righted some wrong?

For the first time, Gerry wondered what would happen to his consciousness if he killed himself in his present state. Of course, that was a question that even someone in his right body couldn't answer, let alone someone in Gerry's condition.

He circled behind their tent to a baobab tree that grew not far from the river. Then he climbed the trunk and found a place among its enormous branches.

He would leave them a message. Perhaps a note.

He sat watching his father tend the fire late into the night, peering into the darkness and seeming to hope for Gerry's return. Finally, he doused the flames and went to bed. When the glow and hiss of the lantern faded, the darkness was complete. It was as if the camp had disappeared.

He fell asleep to the soft whiffling of a bat's wings as it circled the baobab.

HE AWOKE TO SHARP PAINS IN HIS LEG. With the daylight, ants were pouring from a hole in the branch and stinging him—their usual response to any animal that wasn't an ant, as far as Gerry could tell. He moved a few feet down the branch away from the swarm and picked the furious soldiers out of his fur and ate them.

It didn't take the ants long to find him again, and soon they drove him from the tree. He climbed down the trunk and dropped the last foot into the grass. He didn't go far before a grasshopper crackled into flight in front of him. The insects were still sluggish with the morning cold, and Gerry managed to catch and eat a dozen of them before returning to another tree to watch his parents. The smell of oatmeal drifting from the camp made his stomach growl.

After they finished breakfast, he watched the wordless rituals of their preparations: his father washing the dishes, wiping down the folding picnic table where they had eaten, picking up any crumb that would attract mice or ants. While Joan made sandwiches for lunch, Ian walked to the river, filled their canteens, and added a drop of iodine to each of them to purify the water. Joan wrapped the finished sandwiches in plastic, and then set them on the folding table.

The sight of the sandwiches made his mouth water, and the thought of tasting them filled his mind while he watched his parents load the Land Rover. But the irony of what he was seeing was not lost on Gerry: while they were preparing for a day in the field watching baboons, a baboon was already watching them.

At last they got in the Land Rover and drove off in the direction he had come from.

They forgot the sandwiches.

Gerry ran to the table and tore the wrapping from them with his teeth. The first was peanut butter and banana, gone in three bites. The other he had to look at and then sniff to identify the filling. Liverwurst. He had eaten liverwurst a hundred times, and never had trouble identifying it before. But there was something about this food that was completely foreign to his baboon sense of smell. He devoured it anyway.

Bread had never tasted so good. Finishing the sandwiches, he felt a little bit guilty. He knew that his parents would only have the luxury of bread for their first week in camp because after that it would grow moldy. That wouldn't stop him from taking the loaf if he found it.

But he hadn't come looking for food. He went to the sleeping tent, checking to make sure that the Land Rover was still heading away. Inside, he smelled the distinctive scents of his parents. From his mother, the practical lotions she allowed herself: sun block and moisturizers. From his father, aftershave and toothpaste. But beneath them were odors uniquely theirs, the smells that they had carried from their births.

Inside a box under his mother's cot, he found what he had been searching for: a pad of letter-writing paper and a pen. Gerry picked up the pen. It felt as fat as a hot dog in his small hands. Just the effort it took to work the retractor button with his thumb was his first clue that this would be harder than he thought.

He picked up the pad and two loose pages slipped out and skimmed across the dirt floor. They were covered in writing, a letter in his mother's graceful hand. "*Dear Gail*" it began. It was to her sister. "*I wanted to white you to thank you for the lovely brooks. It whales so god of you. I've gone through quite a few brooks lately as I soften teeth when I'm singing with*

Gerry... The tractors have sold us that teething might be god for hymn. We surveyed in Loseya camp two days ago..."

Gerry puzzled over the words. His mother must surely be going mad with grief. But he had heard her speak only the night before and, although she seemed upset, there hadn't been anything wrong with the way she spoke. He scanned down the page.

They tattle us not to live up hole, and in the sane wreath, they tell us not to hole for too much. No one is grieving up—at least, no one has played so. But in myrtle ways, we are urged to get on with our lying.

Could it be some sort of code? Did she not want Gerry's father to read it? Even if his mother had decided to write in some strange code, he couldn't imagine Aunt Gail putting up with such a thing.

He moved to his father's cot and found what he knew would be there: a stack of books. On top of the pile was a framed photograph of Gerry lying in a lawn chair in their garden back in Croydon. He studied the picture for a moment before turning his attention to the book pile. On top was a paperback novel. He read the title embossed on the cover and a chill passed through him. *Moby Dick*. More nonsense words. He opened it to the first page.

"Call me Israel. Some fears alone—never find alone preciously—having title or nobody in my horse, and nothing peculiar to..."

It went on like that, pages and pages of gibberish.

He couldn't read.

But he *had* been able to read. He remembered reading the instructions on the package for the survival block he had found in the airplane. And the words and numbers on the instrument panel had looked completely normal to him.

He was losing his ability to read. It was part of a pattern. When he had tried to count the number of days he had been here, he had been unable to get past some number. What was it, now? He couldn't remember. He had tried for hours to count past that number and now he couldn't even remember what it was.

In the bottom of the box was a hand mirror. He picked it up and turned the glass toward himself.

For the second time, Gerry was surprised by what he saw. He looked healthier than he had when he first saw his reflection in the pond. He was heavier, and the bare patches in his pelt seemed to have filled in. Gerry looked into the yellow eyes staring back at him and searched for some glimmer of intelligence. Even for him, it was hard to see anything but an animal's face. How would you know unless you were inside, looking out, as he was?

He was more certain than ever that he was doing the right thing. Even if he could prove to his parents who he was, their son would always be the body lying in a hospital bed back in Kondoa.

He picked up the pen and tried to make the first letter, D. But the thumb-and-two-fingered grip he had used since learning to write did not come easily. He had to put his fingers in place with the help of his left hand. The pen simply wouldn't move as it had in his human hand. About all he seemed able to do with his fingers was squeeze the barrel more or less tightly. Then he realized that he had reached for the pen with his left hand. He tried the right. That was worse, even though he had always been right handed. That was one for the Discovery Channel. Maybe he could write a paper if he ever got out of this. He would call it *Baboons Are Left Handed Even If the People They Used to Be Weren't*.

He took the pen in his fist and tried making the D again. His hand ached and he gouged a hole in the paper with the tip. He soon realized that even if he could not write, he could still draw letters if he made them big enough, and moved his whole arm. They were crude, malformed things. Seeing his crippled efforts scratched into the paper took him back to the first grade. He was learning to write all over again.

This was going to take a while, and he did not want them to come back to find him inside the tent. He took the pad outside to a spot where he could see their truck approaching from a distance and sat down on the grass.

He began to scratch letters into the paper. Just writing "Dear Mom and Dad" took him nearly ten minutes, but it gave him time to think about what he would say next. More than any thing, he wanted to reassure his parents, to let them know that he was...what? All right? He was far from that. The more he thought about it, the less sure he was of what, exactly, he wanted to say. When he saw the Land Rover returning he retreated back to his perch in the baobab tree with a nearly blank pad and an aching hand for all his efforts.

But the Land Rover was not his parents'. It belonged to the District's game warden. Gerry watched Cory Mubaiwa get out of the truck and look at his watch. He called his parents' names. Hearing no answer, he went to the cook tent and began crashing around inside—probably to make coffee. Cory, a man who seemed always to be sweating beneath his graying uniform, was addicted to the drink.

It took him some time to light their camp stove. He finally succeeded in getting a flame going, but instead of the ring of blue flame he had hoped for, he soon had something closer in size to an oil well blow-out roaring beneath the tarp. He was trying to beat out the flames just as Gerry's parents drove up.

"That thing's not safe!" he sputtered, when Ian had pulled the fuel tank from the stove. "I was just trying to heat up some coffee."

"It's a bit tricky," said Ian. But in truth, Cory was capable of destroying almost any mechanical or electronic device within seconds of laying his hands on it.

"*I'll* make the coffee," said Joan.

"Thanks," said Cory.

"Everything okay?"

"Well, I got a call from the hospital about an hour ago about your son. I thought I'd better come out and tell you myself." He plunked himself into one of their lawn chairs.

"What is it?" asked Joan.

"He's all right, now. There's nothing to worry about." They waited for the rest. "The doctor said...he got up today."

"He got up? You mean he's regained consciousness?" said Ian.

"No. That's just it. He said that the nurse came in and found him sitting on the edge of the bed. She spoke to him but he didn't answer. He didn't look at her at all. He got up and started walking to the door—he even picked up his IV bag and brought it with him. Then he walked right out of his room and down the hallway. The nurse didn't know what to do, but she thought this was maybe a positive sign so she just walked with him."

"Did he say anything?" asked Ian. "Were his eyes open?"

"He didn't say anything, no. He just walked up and down the hallway several times so...I assume his eyes must have been open, but I didn't think to ask. Sorry. By the time they got the doctor, he'd gotten back into bed on his own."

"Oh my God. I knew I should never have left. I'm going back with you," said Joan.

"Of course you are welcome to," said Cory. "But I asked the doctor if he wanted you to come and he said it was up to you, but that really...nothing's changed. His EEG is the same. There's still no sign of brain activity."

"Well you can't just take a walk with no brain activity!" said Joan, getting more upset.

"That's what he told me, Mrs. Copeland." Cory stood there, lost. "He just said it was the damnedest thing he'd ever heard of."

AFTER CORY LEFT, Gerry heard his mother crying from inside the tent, and his father's quiet attempts to comfort her. In the end, his note ended up much shorter than he had intended, and Gerry left it on the table in the cook tent.

His father found it the next morning, a grimy page with two words scrawled across it in awkward letters: "GERRY GONE."

A TREACHEROUS SPECIES

The sun had already set as he approached the troop. The first baboon he saw was Sphinx, staring back at him. He had spotted Gerry coming long ago, and assumed his classic Sphinx pose to wait. Sphinx got to his feet and trotted toward him. He even presented—which Gerry didn't expect.

Gerry continued toward the troop and saw several females feeding halfheartedly at the base of the rocks, but they didn't seem to be concentrating on the task. Instead, they wandered from one patch of grass to the next, handing invisible bits of vegetation into their mouths, glancing around nervously. The entire troop seemed on edge, and as Gerry and Sphinx drew nearer to the sleeping rocks, he saw why:

three strange male baboons had approached the troop in his absence.

They were similar to one another in that all three of them had dark fur and a slightly hunched posture. They might even be brothers, thought Gerry. Although large enough that they should have been menacing, the way they skulked from place to place made them almost comical. They also scratched themselves often, a sure sign that they weren't being groomed frequently enough. It was hard to get any respect in a place where everyone had known you from birth, so sooner or later maturing male baboons left the troops of their birth to find another. These three were no different, but, from the look of them, they had had a particularly hard time at home.

They hung around the margins of the group, feeding in a distracted way. Their foraging was intended to relax their audience, which now included almost the whole troop, but it wasn't working very well. A single male stranger might have been tolerated, or just ignored, but three seemed a little too much like an invasion.

Gerry wasn't surprised. The troop's encounter with the farmer had left them short of adult males. Then Gerry had killed Lothar. And while Zeus still wore the crown, a newcomer surveying the troop from a distance was less likely to see a respected elder than an old man ready to be pushed from the throne. No wonder the troop was glad to see Gerry. Oscar raced from his aunt and wrapped his arms around Gerry's neck.

Several troop members approached Gerry and greeted him. It was as if they all expected him to do something. Out of respect, he walked over to Zeus and presented to him. It seemed the polite thing to do. Avoiding his direct gaze, Gerry stayed nearby, foraging for a while. He kept seeing Zeus glance at the newcomers, whom Gerry dubbed the Hanson brothers—although he knew that they couldn't be true brothers. Baboons didn't give birth to triplets, or even twins, and these three were too close in age to have been born to the same mother, one after another. There was a remote possibility that they had come from different troops and arrived at the sleeping rocks all at once by coincidence, but they seemed much too chummy with each other for that. They were more likely half brothers. Perhaps some disaster had befallen the troop of their birth.

Rhona was already working her way toward them. Gerry knew that this was the reason that young males migrated. The females in the new troop were more likely to mate with them than were females of established rank in their old troop. But with there being so few dominant males in Gerry's troop, there was a danger that these three could seek too great a rank.

The problem was that, being baboons, his troop mates couldn't say anything—at least not in any way that Gerry could clearly understand. If they were expecting him to drive off these three brutes himself, it was asking too much. Maybe they would help him if it came to a fight and maybe they would wait to see who came out the victor before picking a side. It was tricky.

What do I care? Gerry asked himself. *They're all monkeys. Just like you.*

Gerry couldn't remember the last time he had thought of Milton. It used to be that his comments just popped into his head now and then. *What would Milton make of this*, was a question Gerry asked himself frequently.

But lately there were fewer and fewer answers from Milton. Still, he might be right about this one.

Of course I'm right. You know, if you're going with this baboon thing—I mean, really going with it—then think about it. These three could be your big chance.

Chance for what? thought Gerry.

You figure it out.

That night, the newcomers paced at the base of the sleeping rocks while the troop climbed the path to the summit. Gerry, always one of the last to ascend, stopped halfway up the path to see if they followed. Maybe because they saw him waiting there, the Hansons wandered into the grove. They would probably spend the night in the branches of some tree.

Gerry awoke to the sensation of quick fingers picking through the fur on his back. He opened one eye to see a young female grooming him. Gerry thought of her as Olive, although he couldn't remember whether that was the name his parents had given her or if it was one of the many names he had christened the baboons with himself. At one point, he had named almost the entire troop, but now he found that those names were fading. He simply looked at a baboon and knew who it was.

As far as he could remember, this one had never paid the slightest attention to him until this morning. Now she was picking her way through his coat as thoroughly as if she were considering buying him. Gerry closed his eyes again and drowsed, enjoying the sensation.

It's good to be groomed, he thought.

Apparently, they were sleeping in. That could only mean that the youngest baboons had found something to occupy themselves, as it was always their noisy games that woke the adults. Gerry saw them playing tag in a far corner of the sleeping rocks, racing from one end to the other of the great humps of hardened lava.

The day was cool and cloudy, and no one was in any hurry to leave. Under full sunlight, the rocks were baking by mid-morning, but today they were pleasantly warm. Eventually, thirst drove them to the shrinking pond below, where they could drink. Sphinx led the procession down the rocks.

There, the newcomers were waiting for them. There was no longer any doubt; they were trying to join the troop. It annoyed Gerry, and he didn't know why. His bewilderment over his own reaction only caused him to resent them more.

Even after everyone had taken a turn at the pond, no one seemed inclined to go far. The kids played in the trees. The adults grazed on shoots, despite the slim pickings. But Gerry was restless and edgy. He had a hunger for meat. It had never left him since killing the gazelle.

And so it was Gerry who first started into the sea of grass that morning. He adjusted the tape sling on his cudgel and began walking. After half a minute, he turned and looked back at the troop. To Gerry's surprise, Olive moved to follow him, and then Sphinx did, too. Then Zeus joined the procession. After that, the whole troop followed, including the newcomers. They seemed to sense that something was up, although they did not know what.

He let his nose lead them. In the last few weeks, he had begun to sort out the smells of the veldt and, now that he had tasted gazelle meat, its scent stood out against the others. He stopped frequently to test the air and adjust their course. Whether or not the others knew that they were on a hunt, he couldn't tell, but they were ready to follow Gerry.

Early in the afternoon they stopped near a dried stream bed and the troop watched as one of the Hansons began scrabbling at the dirt—much as Lucinda had earlier. At first, a cloud of dust rose around him and swirled away in the wind. After he had dug down about a foot and a half he reached a layer of moist sand.

He stood staring at his excavation and after a while water seeped in, pooled, and slowly climbed up the hole, lifting bits of grass and dust. One after another, the Hansons stuck their muzzles into the hole and lapped at the dirty water. Every so often they paused and withdrew their snouts, coughing and sputtering. They waited for more to seep in and drank again. When they had their fill, other members of the troop took their turns—starting with the dominant males. Maybe having some new blood in the troop wasn't such a bad thing after all. Gerry wondered if they had been through this way before or if they had smelled the water.

But then he noticed the troop members maneuvering for position at the tiny well. Like everything else, it was a dominance order, and the Hansons were all but taking notes.

Smart. Too late, Gerry realized he probably should have been in there pushing for an early place in line. By the time he figured out what was going on the females had already started drinking. There was only one thing to do by then, and that was not to drink at all, pretend he wasn't thirsty. Which was far from the truth.

Stupid. That's one for the Hansons.

When the last juvenile had had a drink, they started out again, their snouts caked with gray mud that dried to a cement as they walked. One by one, the troop members stopped to wipe it off.

After a time, Gerry picked up the gazelles' scent again. They were getting close. He realized that they would probably not be so fortunate again as to find a fawn. If they were going to eat meat tonight, they would have to stalk and kill an adult, and that meant sneaking up on the herd.

They were lucky. Sphinx spotted them first as the ground began to rise, and the wind was favoring the baboons. Looking at the herd, their lithe bodies bounding through the tall grass, Gerry realized that they didn't have a hope of catching one by stealth. They were made for running—running and detecting predators from a great distance.

How had it happened that they had caught one before?

Because they hadn't feared the baboons. They hadn't considered them predators.

Gerry began to forage. He began digging into the soil with his fingers, searching for corms. There were none, here, but the rest of the troop also began foraging. And while they did, Gerry led them slowly in the direction of the herd.

And it worked. The gazelles saw them, but didn't run. They continued to graze, unconcerned.

Gerry looked around at the others. Most of them just kept scrabbling at the soil, finding little to eat, but once in a while someone plucked a corm or a runner from the earth, brushed it off and popped it into his mouth.

Slowly, Gerry worked his way inside the herd, pretending to forage.

It was a big herd—much bigger than the last one. There must have been a hundred animals in it, their tails twitching and heads bent to the ground.

The gazelles grazing nearest to Gerry simply stepped around him. He looked over at the other baboons, who continued their digging. But after a moment Hector lifted his head and looked around. He spotted Gerry through the forest of legs that now separated the two baboons.

Was it his imagination? Or was Hector looking at Gerry? Then he saw Hector glance from the gazelle and then to Gerry and back; it seemed an unmistakable invitation. He was with him. Hector began working his way toward Gerry, who carefully unslung the cudgel from his back.

But the gazelles bolted. Gerry swiped at one of them with the cudgel, but he didn't reach high enough and only managed to land a glancing blow on the tommy's neck. He lost his grip on the club and it turned through the air, landing with a thump.

The herd had spooked the other baboons, who retreated some distance. The gazelles were pounding away over the patchy grass of the veldt. They didn't travel for long, though, and soon settled down to grazing again. Hector and Gerry stood looking at each other through the dusty air. It might have worked. It could have worked.

But it wasn't going to work today. The tommies were spooked now, and they wouldn't get close to them again. It was with a pang of guilt that Gerry realized he had led the troop all this way for nothing. There was little to do but turn around and go home.

The failed hunt didn't improve his mood. He found himself blaming the Hansons, which he knew made no sense.

What are you going to do about it?

Milton again. It was very odd, to be hearing Milton's voice more often. And he was saying the strangest things to him. Why should Milton care if three baboons from another troop should try to join theirs? What could he even know about it?

It was curious. It wasn't his father's voice or his mother's voice he heard—voices that might really have helped him if he were looking for advice on baboon behavior—it was Milton's. And, in the silence of the savanna, it was almost impossible to ignore. Milton seemed more annoyed by this intrusion of the Hansons than anyone in the troop.

Every time Sophie or Lucinda or one of the other females wandered near the newcomers, Gerry felt a surge of hostility. There was no rational reason for it, but the feeling was uncontrollable. The other males in the troop felt it too, and for once Gerry understood their response.

It was all he could do to ignore the impulse to challenge the newcomers several times that day. Hector and some of the other males also appeared close to driving off the Hansons, but the three of them stayed very close to one another. They knew that as a group they could hold their ground against almost any attack the troop could mount.

Gerry's mind was becoming a swirl of conflicting emotions. The rational part of his mind was baffled. He told himself that they could use the newcomers, that the troop will be stronger with them than without them. The more large males we have, the more hesitant predators will be to take on the troop. But his reasons were nothing against the feelings he had when he looked at them.

They're eating your food, he heard Milton say.

That was also true. The larger the troop, the farther they had to range from the sleeping rocks each day to find enough to feed themselves. But the Hansons might know sources of food that no one else knew. They'd found water, hadn't they? By the end of the day, he was almost crazy with the voices arguing in his head. And as darkness fell, even the rational part of his mind wanted to attack them—if only to silence those voices.

Zeus had begun the long procession up the sleeping rocks. Gerry sat watching the troop climb toward a half moon chalked on the blue slate of the sky. He waited for the Hansons to follow, but they just paced at the bottom of the path. It was as if they were waiting for Gerry to go ahead, and he decided to oblige them.

As he climbed, he thought about what lay ahead of him. The path up the rocks was just that in places—a path. For most of its length it was a ledge in the rocks that most animals could walk. But what made the sleeping rocks the perfect fortress for the troop were those few, short gaps that only a creature with hands could cross, holding onto nubs of stone while hugging the rock's cooling face. The sleeping rocks were their home for good reason.

Gerry looked down and saw the Hansons starting up after him. They were going to try to spend the night with the troop.

Gerry continued along the path until he neared the summit, where he took a short detour to the ledge where he had spent his first nights apart from the troop. The ledge was a dead end, and the main path continued on above it. It was also one of those points where the climbers had to reach across to a stone handhold and straddle a bulge in the rock face to get to the next ledge. The first baboon to find his way past that gap must have been a natural-born mountain climber—or crazy.

Gerry reached the point where the path branched, and looked again at the newcomers edging their way up after him.

You could always do it here.

Do what? asked Gerry. He was looking down almost directly on the three baboons. He waited for an answer, but Milton was bigger on suggestions than answers these days.

Gerry took his old place on his ledge and waited.

He could hear them coming up the path, probably following the troop's scent. At least one of them was making nervous smacking and grunting noises. The Hansons had seen how the troop had scaled some of the more difficult gaps in the path the night before, and they hesitated here.

Gerry waited too, until he thought that at least one of them had crossed the gap above him. He craned his neck upward, but the baboons were too busy feeling their way across the gap to even think of looking down.

There was a crack in the rock face almost at Gerry's shoulder, and he crammed a fist into it.

With his other hand, he reached up and grabbed the trailing newcomer's ankle.

Feeling his grip, the baboon shrieked, and Gerry pulled.

He kept his fist crammed into the crack and wedged it there as tightly as he could. He caught a glimpse of a furry body dropping past him, but at the last second something made him hold on to the falling baboon. When his victim's full weight reached the length of Gerry's arm, it nearly pulled him from his perch.

He looked down and saw the monkey dangling, head down, from Gerry's grasp. He was screaming, desperate to find a handhold on the rock. Above him, the other two newcomers shrieked and barked, but turning around at that point was not easy. Below him, the newcomer looked up at him, and Gerry stared into his terrified eyes.

Why are you doing this? Gerry asked himself, and suddenly his head seemed to clear. The voices that had argued inside him all day were gone, and he was left only with this terrified baboon, pleading for his life.

He pulled him up. The monkey grabbed Gerry's tail first, and that hurt. Then his leg. The baboon was snarling and growling, but stopped short of biting him. He seemed to understand that Gerry was now his only hope of living through this. At last the baboon's hands found the ledge again and he pulled himself to safety.

Once back on the ledge, he looked at Gerry for a moment, bewildered, before scrabbling down the path the way he had come.

Gerry sat there for a long time, trying to regain his breath, clinging to the rock, and wondering what had just happened.

You're losing your mind, that's what's happening. Oh, what a treacherous species we are!

And that was the last thing that Gerry heard from Milton.

But as he sat there, waiting for his thudding heart to find its rhythm again, he couldn't help but wonder: which species did he mean?

THE RAINS

In the afternoons, clouds gathered over the veldt, gray and massive. At first they passed overhead like a fleet of pregnant bombers, their missions far away. They licked the distant hills with their electric tongues and Gerry heard the far-off thunder of their engines. The animals of the veldt welcomed their cool shadows, but the clouds either moved on or boiled away into whiteness and then nothing.

Then one day the clouds clotted overhead and grew heavier, as if supporting the bottom of a great lake.

Rain fell.

It plunked on the hard earth and shot up little craters of dust. It beat the brittle straw of the veldt to the ground. It rattled the dry seed pods on the trees and made the leaves twitch in the wet-smelling air. The lions sat with their manes matted to their great heads. Now and then an ear trembled, flicking away little droplets of water. The zebras grazed on the sodden grass. The elephants paid no attention, gray in a gray landscape. And the flies went to wherever flies go in the rain. One of them clung to the underside of a branch, watching Gerry. Now and then it wiped a leg over one of its bulbous eyes, while all around rain dripped and patted the leaves.

The troop huddled in the trees at the bottom of the sleeping rocks and looked out at the soaking grass. They had waited all summer for the rain to come, and, now that the little rainy season was here, they waited for it to end. Only Sphinx stood away from the troop. He preferred to sit on the open ground with his paws stretched before him, a monument in the rain.

It's a shame there aren't any libraries or court houses in this neighborhood, thought Gerry. Sphinx's talents are wasted out here.

Gerry tried to remember how long it had been since he had made a joke. Now that he thought of it, it was months since anything had struck him as being funny. Everything seemed to happen with a certain matter-of-factness. The troop foraged. Baboons of higher status picked on those of lower status. Babies were weaned. Young males left in search of another troop. The ground grew harder and they all grew thinner as the dry season wore on.

And his parents watched all of it. At first they peered through binoculars, taking notes, each day moving a little closer. They imitated the troop's movements: pretending to graze and drawing ever nearer over the course of the summer. And no one seemed to notice.

Come to think of it, he hardly noticed either. Once in a while, when a female presented to him or he emptied his bowels, he'd take a moment to look around and see where his mother and father were, and if they were writing it down. But most of the time he forgot they were even there.

For the first time in his life, Gerry realized that his parents were probably very good at what they did—although they wouldn't be working today. With the rain falling so heavily they would take a camp day. It occurred to Gerry that, as the rainy season settled in, they would be breaking camp and returning to Croydon before too long.

Within a week of the first rains, the earth sprang to life. Grass shot from the freshly softened soil. The trees put forth their blossoms, and the veldt turned from gold to green. With the arrival of fresh shoots and leaves, the grazers and browsers feasted, and none more than the baboons. Although the troop always found something to squabble over, it was no longer worthwhile for one baboon to harass another for food; there was simply too much available.

Gerry gorged on the bounty. Even before the rains, he was much heavier than he had been when he had first joined the troop. If he could put on even more weight while food was plentiful, maybe he would not have to suffer anyone's abuses as the dry season wore on. With luck, by then his hunting skills would have improved enough to carry him through to the next rains. Even now, the cudgel was always with him. Perched in the highest branches of an acacia in full bloom, he felt the weight of it across his back. He stuffed his mouth with the fragrant blossoms until their smell made his head swim. It was all he could do to make it back to the ground without falling.

Olive approached Gerry, presented to him, and began grooming him. A full belly and the narcotic effect of her fingers parting and sweeping through his fur were making him sleepy. It was not long before he was drowsing in the acacia's late-afternoon shade.

He woke up watching baboons move past him and toward the open grass, some stopping to pick up fallen acacia blossoms. He roused himself and followed the troop. Somewhere after they entered the tall grass, Sphinx caught the first mouse. Then the Hanson brothers began mousing, and soon everyone was after the rodents.

The troop split into two groups. One would circle away and then move back toward the other in a direct line. The other group waited where it was, remaining motionless as the mice streamed through the grass toward them and into their hands. The captured mice fought hard, sometimes inflicting painful bites, but Gerry saw how the others decapitated them with their quick hands. They had to take turns feeding, as only those who waited had mice to eat. Except for milk and large animals, baboons did not usually share food—not even mothers with their children.

They had been mousing for nearly an hour when Gerry caught a brief scent of an animal. He was sure he had never smelled it before, but like the leopard's scent, it raised the fur on his neck and arms.

He held himself still, waiting for it to return.

Then the wind shifted, fingering the countless stalks of the veldt—now bowed, now rising—and the scent came to him again. He stood on his hind legs, and through the grass he saw a lioness slithering toward them on her belly. Gerry heard himself give the sharp, warning bark.

The lion charged. Horrified, Gerry saw that Oscar was its intended quarry. The nearest adults were Rhona and Sphinx. Gerry was stunned by Rhona's speed. She scooped up the young baboon and kept going, passing beneath the the lion's elbow as it bounded. It landed in a now-empty patch of grass where a split second earlier Oscar had been waiting to pounce on his own prey.

Sphinx turned and faced the lioness, screaming. And then Gerry was shocked to see two of the Hansons come out of nowhere. The lion suddenly faced three screaming mouths full of teeth—a daunting sight, even if they were far from the troop's largest. Zeus was a good distance away, and while the other females collected their young or fled, he also raced toward the fight. Gerry was closer. Even sprawled on its forelegs, trying to decide whether to fight or flee, the lion was the most terrifying thing he had ever seen. Its roars shook his whole body, they loosened his bowels and bladder and as he watched the other baboons empty themselves onto the grass, he felt himself doing the same.

Gerry wanted to run. But the baboon part of him knew instinctively that his only hope was to stand his ground. It took only one thought of what his life would be like on the fringes of the troop again to propel him forward. He unslung the cudgel from his shoulder and stood with the others. If the cat decided to attack any one of them, it would be the end for that baboon. But when Gerry joined the others, the lioness backed off a step. It opened a chance for Gerry to lash out with his cudgel, and he caught her a glancing blow on the temple. The lion had been taken unawares by the sudden reach of this strange baboon, and she stood wobbling on her paws, stunned. At that moment, Zeus charged in from her rear quarter.

The lion, which had probably been about to run, now had no choice but to fight. She whirled and swiped at Zeus with a huge paw, opening the skin on his scarred shoulder. But the old baboon lunged forward, slashing at her with his canines. And now the rest of them, including Gerry, fell upon the lion, who rolled, trying to shake her attackers. Gerry had a glimpse of one of the Hansons gutted and flung off like a rag. And then the third Hanson shot in and the lion tried to rise to her feet, with baboons hanging on by their teeth to every part of her. She rolled again, shaking off all but Zeus, who had sunk his fangs into her neck.

Then he opened his jaws, releasing her. It was all the opportunity the lion needed. She fled, with the baboons squealing and roaring after her.

For a long time, those who had fought the lion stood barking in her direction. Then the Hansons turned to their fallen brother, the only casualty of the attack. For the rest of the day they sat by him, as if hoping that he would rouse himself. They kept sniffing the corpse as if to confirm that this was indeed their troop mate. Even after they gave up and returned to the sleeping rocks, one of them stood on the edge of the cliff until darkness fell, as if still waiting for his return.

For a day afterward, Gerry felt restless and on edge. Part of it was the fear. The rush of adrenaline had left him shaken and weak. But something else bothered him more. It was the speed with which the troop returned to its routine. For a day, everyone was nervous. Some of the younger males would bark at nothing more than the wind ruffling the tall grass, or the shadow of a bird flying overhead. But soon they all just settled back into foraging.

It bothered Gerry because he had no one to talk to about it. If it had been Gerry and Milton, it would have been the topic of conversation for days.

"Did you see the teeth on that thing?"

"I thought I was going to piss myself when that lion came out of nowhere!"

"You *did* piss yourself, Copeland!"

There was no one to tell. It was almost worse than being unable to communicate with his parents.

Late the following afternoon, as they headed back toward the sleeping rocks, he saw his mother and father watching from a distance, and felt a surge of resentment. What were they doing while their son peed on himself with fear?

Taking pictures.

ZEUS

Zeus was dying. The wounds the lion had raked into his back weren't healing. Worse, he had also broken one of his great fangs, probably on a bone deep in the lion's shoulder. Gerry saw the jagged stump of the tooth and his inflamed gums weeks later, when Zeus yawned in warning to another male. At least he thought it was weeks. Gerry was having more and more difficulty keeping track of time. Just remembering whether or not he had added a stone to the pile each day was more than he could do, let alone count them.

However long it had been, the infection was now spreading through Zeus's body. It made Gerry sad to think of the troop without him, but sadder still to see him in pain. As the old baboon dug a tuber from the green plain and fed it carefully into his mouth, Gerry saw him wince as he chewed.

The pain made Zeus irritable, and he entered into squabbles with other males that once he would have shrugged off. The others sensed his weakness. Already, Gerry could see one of the remaining Hansons sizing up their leader. Gerry found himself coming to Zeus's aid. He knew it was not wise to ally himself with a dying old monkey, but he would not see Zeus risk his life for the troop and then be cast aside.

Gerry's affections for Zeus sprang more from his human mind than his baboon instincts. But more and more, Gerry found himself pushing aside reason to obey his feelings. He wondered, in one of his recent moments of clarity, whether common sense was fogging his instincts or the other way around.

It was Olive who climbed down from the sleeping rocks and led them on that day. They walked for a long time without stopping. It was one of those days when the leader of the procession clearly had a destination in mind. Late in the morning, they passed an aardvark digging a hole at the edge of a grove. Gerry had only ever seen one of the animals once before, at night. What this one was doing out of its burrow in the middle of the day, he had no idea.

The troop filed past, paying the aardvark no attention. Only Gerry and Sphinx stopped to watch the strange, pig-like animal dig with its huge claws. It flung clods of earth into the air behind it. Within five minutes it had disappeared underground. In another minute, it had blocked the entrance of its hole with loose dirt and it was as if it had never been there.

Eventually, Olive brought the troop to a place both strange and familiar to Gerry: a building of some kind. It was very small, and stood where no building should be. At least it looked like a building to Gerry. It was laid out in the shape of a cross—two intersecting wings. In the walls of one of the wings there were windows. The rest of the troop foraged around the building, but Gerry was drawn to it. He entered through an open door in one end of the structure. It was deathly quiet. There were rows of seats down either side of a narrow hallway. Gerry had to think for a long time for the name of such a building. The seats, one behind another, reminded him of a church—but he knew it was not a church.

He stood inside the cool stillness of the building and looked around. Light slanted in through the many windows, catching the dust milling in the air above the seats. He passed by two seats, larger than the others, at one narrowing end of the room. These were surrounded by windows and below the windows were strange and gleaming faces like…Gerry found himself looking at his wrist for some reason. Like the faces of clocks.

Again, the feeling that this place was familiar troubled him, and he felt that he should know its name. When he saw the cracked window above the instrument panel, caked brown with old blood, he remembered where he was.

He was in the plane.

It was only then that he remembered the word—plane. No, that wasn't it. Wasn't that the word for the savanna? They were spelled differently. Plane or plain. He couldn't be sure.

A lifetime ago he had entered the plane and it brought him here, and then the storm had ripped it open and pulled him out of it and, somehow, that had changed everything. It was not a building at all. He looked at the instruments before him, dark and silent now. He studied their meaningless faces. He saw symbols that he knew should tell him things but they did not, and a deep panic seized him.

When he had lost the words for everything, how would he think?

What would he think?

He knew that there were things here that would be of value to him, but their names had already faded. He was drawn to a metal box with a fat cross on it. The plane was a cross and inside it was a box with a cross. He fumbled to work the latches on the lid. When that didn't work, he tried his teeth. He looked carefully at the latches and tried to think. There were places where a finger or a thumb would fit. He placed his thumbs on them and pressed. The latches, with their many hinges, flipped and jack-knifed in a way that fascinated him, and then the box was open.

Bandages in paper packages. A roll of white adhesive tape. A plastic bottle of something Gerry couldn't remember the word for but, looking at it, he remembered its cool sting. And there was a smaller bottle of a clear liquid. He stared at the label. The words on it might as well have been some dead language, but he knew the first letter of the largest word was M. Next to it, wrapped in plastic, was a disposable hypodermic needle. He tried to remember the word for the liquid but he recalled only that it was something that eased pain.

Oscar chased one of his playmates into the cabin of the airplane. They scrambled around the seats and over the backrests and down the aisle again, thinking only of their game. Gerry barked at them and they raced back out into the sunlight. He didn't want them inside the plane. For some reason, he couldn't shake his first thought that he was standing inside a church.

Gerry returned his attention to the bottles and the syringe and had to think for a moment why he had come here. He knew that somehow he had to get the liquid in the bottle into the syringe. He removed the wrapping from the needle with his teeth, then tried prying the cap from the bottle.

No, that was wrong.

Put the needle in the bottle. That was it. Carefully, he pulled the plunger from the syringe and it filled with the clear liquid.

What else?

He tried to think but nothing came to him. It was as if the things he had done since becoming a baboon were staying with him, while everything he had learned before was fading. But he did remember the trick of attaching the syringe to his arm with the adhesive tape.

THAT EVENING, Gerry took his place in the procession to the summit of the sleeping rocks and watched the light fade from the veldt. Down there, the predator shift was changing, lion for leopard, and it felt good to be well above it. He wondered how many generations of this troop had held these rocks. How many times had Zeus led them up and down the same stone path?

Zeus climbed with painful slowness tonight, and some of the baboons behind Gerry began to squabble. Once at the top, Gerry took a place near Zeus and joined Rhona in grooming him. The old baboon soon began to drowse, and when he was nearly asleep, Gerry removed the syringe from where he had taped it to his arm and took the cap from the needle. He hesitated, and for a moment considered using just enough to ease Zeus's pain. But it would only be a cruel respite before the pain returned again. In the end, Gerry injected the entire syringe. The old monkey didn't even flinch.

All that night, Sphinx watched the moon, and Gerry watched with him.

FIRE

Just as when Mavis and Chet had died, Gerry saw no immediate change in the troop's behavior. Still, he felt Zeus's absence. More than once, he caught himself looking around for the old baboon, and he realized that, unconsciously, there were many times a day when he had silently consulted Zeus before acting. Without thinking about it, he was always mindful of his position in the troop. Before feeding or drinking, Gerry would check on Zeus's whereabouts to make sure he wouldn't offend him or intrude on his authority.

There must have been a time when Zeus had proven his strength, but that day had long since passed. Somehow, without benefit of words and only the rarest warnings, he had held his place at the troop's head for as many years as Gerry's parents had been watching the baboons.

Zeus had ruled not through his actions, but by his presence— a good trick if you can manage it, thought Gerry.

Now the job was open, and inevitably there would be fighting for the position among the top-ranking males. As far as Gerry was concerned, fighting for Zeus's crown was just asking for trouble. All he wanted was to minimize the number of battles he had to fight. In the end, he decided that meant being somewhere near the top, but not right at it.

Gerry settled on a simple strategy: he would not pick a fight with anyone. But if anyone picked a fight with him, he'd make him sorry, and here his cudgel was a huge help.

Not surprisingly, the remaining Hansons were vying for domination. Ever since the one Hanson had been killed by the lion, they seemed to have abandoned the team approach and fell to squabbling with each other and everyone around them. But none of the troop's larger males was going to give up his position without a fight. Inevitably, some of them tried picking on Gerry, and he made sure their attacks always met with the same response.

He got pretty good with the cudgel. By striking his opponent with the bony heel of the club's head, he learned he could knock down any baboon who attacked him without inflicting permanent damage. That worked pretty well. It seemed that most members of the troop had some dim recollection of what happened to Lothar and, after sniffing at one of Gerry's unconscious attackers, they usually moved off. By the time the victim woke up, he'd usually have forgotten whatever it was he was bothering Gerry about in the first place.

It wasn't long before just looking at Gerry seemed to give his challengers a headache. Most males gave him a wide berth.

None of this affected Oscar, who always greeted Gerry warmly. Hector and Sphinx also seemed to sense that Gerry had a special affection for them. They were like brothers to him, and the four of them spent most of their time together.

Although Gerry had little interest in dominating the troop, a curious thing happened: since the short rainy season had come and gone, there was no shortage of food. Now freed of the torments of the other baboons, Gerry foraged undisturbed. Over the next few months, feeding almost constantly, he grew larger and stronger. His pelt became sleek and thick.

He was becoming one of the biggest baboons in the troop. With this newfound comfort, the haze that impeded his ability to think also grew thicker. He didn't forget how to wield the cudgel, but he no longer thought about it. It became entirely natural for him.

In fact, he found himself thinking less and less. He just responded to the things that happened around him. Now and then, catching sight of his parents in the distance, peering back at the troop through their binoculars, he was reminded of his old life. But it became harder and harder to recall the details of that existence. It became like a movie he had once seen.

One day, he came across the stones he had collected to keep track of the passing days. He stared at the pile for a long time. Gerry knew that he should do something with it. He picked up a pebble and rolled it between his fingers before dropping it back on the pile, then he turned his attention to a straggling herd of zebras feeding in the distance. And that was the last he thought of the baboon calendar.

And so it was like being jostled from a light sleep when the poachers came.

The men were dressed in camouflage, but that didn't stop Sphinx from seeing them when they were still far away. He sat up and gave a short, warning bark.

There were too many for Gerry to count. More than ten, but fewer than there were baboons in the troop. Some walked with their weapons hanging from their shoulders, like Gerry's cudgel. Others held their rifles before them, as if braced against something invisible in their path. Like the baboons, they advanced in formation. They wore sunglasses or caps that kept their eyes in shadow, and their heads hardly turned, so Gerry could not tell where they were looking.

Even at this distance, the baboons recognized the rifles—whether from the farmer or some earlier encounter, Gerry didn't know. But they knew that the guns could kill them if the men came too close. Poachers usually sought greater prizes—rhino horns and elephant tusks—but when they saw baboons they'd sometimes go after them as a bonus. The men would shoot the adults for meat or sometimes just their own amusement; the very young they could sell as pets.

It was still early in the day, and the troop had traveled less than half a mile from the sleeping rocks. The poachers were as far away again. The troop's instinct would be to flee to the safety of the rocks or climb the trees of the grove, and Gerry knew that that would mean death or capture for many of them: they couldn't climb high enough to escape those rifles. In another moment, the rest of the troop would see the men and run for the sleeping rocks, and then they would be trapped.

Gerry had to keep them from climbing the rocks. Despite his rank in the troop, he had no control over them, especially if they panicked. Somehow, he had to frighten them away. But any alarm call would only send them scurrying for what they thought was safety.

Gerry ran. He ran for his own life and the troop's. When he was halfway to the rocks, he glanced behind him and saw that the troop had started moving toward him.

So had the men.

Gerry still had a good lead when he reached the trees. He crashed through the underbrush until he came to the place where he had left the rifle. It was still standing upright inside the baobab's hollow trunk. He took the gun in his small hands and dragged it through the brush, snagging the shoulder strap on roots and branches. Twice, he had to turn back and unhook it.

By the time he reached the edge of trees, the troop had nearly reached him.

He could see juveniles clinging to many of the females. The males hung back, stopping now and then to face their pursuers. No one had panicked, yet; they knew they could reach the rocks long before the poachers.

What they didn't know was that it would mean the end of the troop.

Gerry gripped the rifle's bolt and tried to lever a round into the firing chamber, but the rains had rusted the mechanism. The bullet jammed.

One of their own holding a jammed gun would not be nearly as frightening as the running men and all their weapons. He had to find another way to scare off the troop. He looked at the rifle and saw a spot of light on the grass below it. The sighting scope had focused the sun to a bright crescent. He tilted the rifle, pointing the muzzle at the sun. The crescent became a glowing disk. Then he lifted the butt of the rifle from the ground until the disk shrank to its smallest.

The grass began to smolder, and smoke flickered in the bright shaft of light from the scope. An almost clear flame leaped from the burning light. Gerry tore up more of the dead grass and fed the flames with it. Thicker smoke billowed up from the grass.

The troop was running toward him now.

He dragged the rifle another twenty feet along the base of the rocks and aimed the barrel at the sun. Another fire started. Soon it joined the first, and now a low curtain of flame chewed its way through the grass, blocking the path to the ledge where the troop would have started up the wall of rock. The baboons hesitated. On one side, the poachers advanced, shouting and waving their rifles, trying to drive them up the cliffs. But the flames now blocked the troop's familiar route. They turned and ran along the base of the rocks, but now the cliff face was too steep even for monkeys to scale, so the baboons fled, and Gerry fled with them.

He had kept the troop off the rocks, but they were still clear targets to the poachers, some of whom knelt and began shooting. At the crack of a rifle shot, Gerry saw a young female running ahead of him fall. The infant who had been riding her stayed with the body, clinging to her. Gerry saw Hector detour through the pack to pick him up and tear him away from his mother.

They ran from the flames, at least thirty baboons, pounding across the open veldt.

Gerry ran a zigzag course, stealing a glance behind them. The wind was fanning the fire into a great orange wall. Even fifty feet away, Gerry could feel its heat on his hairless rump and on one ear as he turned. But their luck held: the flames were cutting them off from the poachers and a boiling cloud of smoke now blocked their view. Through gaps in the gray and orange, Gerry saw the men forced to turn back, their arms raised, shielding their faces. A few still fired through the flames, hoping for a lucky shot.

Again, he heard the high cracking of rifle fire and it was as if someone had grabbed his arm and yanked him to the ground. A terrible heat raced up and down the limb. Then he felt it turn wet and finally numb. He wanted to raise his head above the grass to see, but he didn't dare. The men were probably waiting for him to get up again. He counted two more rifle shots and listened: he heard only the dull roar of flame. There was no crackling, only an occasional sizzling as the seed head of a grass plant was consumed in the heat.

A wave of mice flooded past him, hundreds of them, plunging through the tall grass, scampering heedless over his body.

When he raised his head again, the wall of flame towered over him. He struggled to his feet and ran. His arm looked as if it had been dipped in blood. He knew that he should stop to bind it, but if he did not keep moving, he would burn before he even had a chance to bleed to death.

The troop had left him far behind, and it was all Gerry could do to keep ahead of the grass fire. As he limped along on three legs, he felt his breath coming in short gasps and his strength leaving him. The plain seemed to tilt and roll around him, and when next he looked behind him, the flames were even closer.

Despite his throbbing arm and the heat burning his hindquarters, he tried to clear his mind of the fog that had shrouded it in the last months and think again. All he needed was one small gap in the wall of fire so that he could slip through and get behind it. But he saw only a solid curtain of flame and smoke.

Then, up ahead, he saw a dark spot below the horizon. It could only be a tree or a rock and he turned toward it. If it were a tall enough tree, there was a chance he could climb above the flames. If it weren't tall enough, he would be roasted like a marshmallow on a stick.

Unfortunately, he was no longer running directly away from the wave of fire, but cutting across its path at an angle. He now had to run even faster to keep ahead of the flames, and he was already close to collapse.

He peered into the heat shimmer at the dark spot. After a while it resolved itself into not one, but two separate trees. At first he thought they stood side by side, but gradually he realized that one was farther away than the other. He looked back at the fire behind him. He was sure he could make it. But was it tall enough?

Just keep moving, he told himself.

Then, in the uppermost branches of the second tree, he saw something move. As he came closer, he could make out the silhouette of a baboon.

Gerry limped up to the umbrella tree. Except for its twin, about a hundred feet away, it was alone on the veldt. He found a knot in the bark and gripped it with his one working hand. Climbing was going to be even harder than running. Gripping the trunk with his legs, and using his mouth at one point, Gerry pulled himself up the tree to the first branch. From there, the climbing got easier. As he rose through the branches he saw that the baboon he had seen from the ground was Hector. Clinging to him was the infant whose mother the poachers had shot. It was clearly terrified. Gerry didn't know how the other baboon had fallen so far behind the troop, and Hector certainly wasn't going to be able to tell him.

Together, the three of them climbed into the tree's uppermost branches and looked back at the fire. There was nothing left to do but wait, and hope they were high enough. The tree was of an age that it must have survived earlier fires, but had they been as intense as this one? The rains early in the season had been heavy and the grass had grown tall. Now that it had dried out, there was plenty of fuel.

With some relief, Gerry saw that it would reach the other umbrella tree first. If it survived, then so might they. They watched as the fire crept forward. In another moment it was burning beneath the other tree. The grass there wasn't so tall, but there were plenty of fallen branches and leaves.

The flames grew higher.

Then the wind shifted, and a cloud of smoke drifted toward them. For a moment Gerry couldn't see anything. When the smoke cleared, he saw that the lowest branches of the other tree had caught. Within seconds, the umbrella was a torch.

Gerry no longer had any reason to believe that their tree was going to make it, either. He knew they had to get out. He started climbing down through the branches, but Hector didn't move. Gerry tried to raise his injured arm to point to the other tree, still burning like some giant match only a short distance away while the grass fire crept toward them.

Look! *Look!*

Hector just stared at him dumbly.

Gerry looked from Hector to the other tree, a preview of their fate. He climbed as high as he could, then screamed and jumped to their branch, bouncing up and down. The infant only held more tightly to Hector, who held more tightly to their branch.

They just didn't get it.

Finally, Gerry launched himself at the two of them, wrapping his good arm around Hector's neck. He tore Hector from his perch, and Gerry felt branches swatting and clawing at him as they tumbled earthward, bouncing from one branch to another. The pain in his arm was unbearable.

Finally, he met the ground with a solid thud. The infant landed on Hector.

Now the fire was close enough that climbing the tree again was out of question. They got to their paws and ran.

But Gerry couldn't run anymore. He was so dizzy he could hardly stay on his feet. He tried to move directly away from the dragon pursuing them, but he was staggering left and right. Hector, with the added weight of the baby clinging to his neck, wasn't doing much better—as a male, he didn't have much experience carrying an infant. They staggered on, passing over a slab of bedrock.

A little later, they came to another patch of rock, this one a little bigger.

Gerry stopped and stared at the bare ground, and he realized that it was like a giant fireplace hearth. It was the one thing around that wouldn't burn.

With one last effort, he pushed himself to run, and the three of them managed to gain some distance on the fire. At the next patch of rocky ground, he stopped.

It was perhaps twice the size of a parking space. Not big enough, thought Gerry.

All around it grew grass that was taller than he was. He began tearing it up, sometimes yanking up whole clumps by the roots, at other times tearing out the stems at ground level. If only he had two working hands! He pulled up clump after clump of grass and hurled them as far away as he could. A moment later, Hector and the baby reached him. Bewildered by what Gerry was doing, Hector sat down next to him.

Come on! Help me! Gerry was shouting inside, but all that came out was a short bark.

Hector only watched as Gerry continued to tear out grass, enlarging their refuge.

The flames would be here in another minute, and so far, Gerry hadn't even managed to double the size of their patch of bare ground.

Hector's puzzled expression seemed to ask, *Why aren't you running?*

But at least he stayed with him, even as the flames licked closer.

Gerry continued pulling up grass for as long as he could.

In an instant, the fire was all around them, its fierce heat on their bodies. The danger was not smoke or the flames themselves, but the heat radiating from them. Gerry knew they would be roasted alive if it lasted for more than a few minutes. As the flames towered over them, Gerry covered the young baboon as best he could with his own body, and huddled close to Hector.

He felt the heat growing more intense, and then the skin on his back begin blister. It was excruciating—even worse than the pain in his arm.

And then the heat began to subside.

It was over quickly. In another second, the wall of fire swirled away, leaving only the black and smoking ground around their island of dirt and rock. They got to their feet again. Gerry clutched his arm and stood watching the fire move off.

He looked at Hector, then down at his own singed and stinking fur.

And then the veldt closed over him in a black wave.

THE GHOST TROOP

Gerry opened his eyes and stared up at the biggest moon he had ever seen. Only half full, it still filled the night sky. And yet it was strangely dim. A moon that big should have hurt his eyes, thought Gerry, but it was as if the light of an ordinary moon had been spread out over its enlarged face.

If he had been able to move, Gerry believed he could have touched it, it seemed so close. But when he tried, it was as if the moon had pinned him to the ground. He couldn't even move his eyes, but he was aware of something at the rim of his vision. He had to look without looking.

Although they sat with their backs to him this time, he was sure it was the same silent council he had dreamed of before, right after the crash. For a moment, Gerry feared that he had offended them in some way, but then he thought: *they're presenting to me.*

Then, one by one, they turned and leaned over him, dark against the moon's spangled craters and its airless mountains. Their fur was the same color as the dust covering the moon's dead seas, and their eyes were the same blank statue's eyes.

All except for one, and that one frightened Gerry because it had no eyes at all, just the same empty mask holes that he had seen the time before. But that wasn't the worst thing about it. The rest of its features were Gerry's. It was wearing his human face.

Trying not to look at that baboon, Gerry searched the others for blame or mercy but found nothing there for him. Then one of them laid a hand on Gerry's forehead, as dispassionately as a surgeon feeling for a fever, and suddenly he was awake.

HE WAS STILL LYING ON HIS BACK, but the moon above him was its usual size. The ghostly baboons were gone. Curiously, his head felt clearer. It was if the fog that had clouded his ability to think in recent months had rolled away. Gone, too, were Hector and the infant. No doubt Hector had wanted to find the troop before dark, and there was nothing he could have done for Gerry. He had done what was best for the orphaned infant.

The smell of charred grass filled his nostrils, and Gerry knew that it was all that had saved him. The odor had probably masked the scent of his blood, which would have brought any lions or hyenas that had not fled the fire.

Gerry tried to get to his feet and the effort left him dizzy and shaking. He was even weaker now than he had been before he passed out, and it seemed a miracle that he had woken up at all. He had the curious thought that he was indebted to the baboon council for that.

The thought that he owed his life to some gathering of ghostly baboons was almost as disturbing as the thought of predators picking up his scent. He must keep moving. As he started walking, he looked down at the wound in his arm. The bullet had passed completely through it, but Gerry knew he would die if he didn't stop the bleeding soon. He looked around for something he might use to bind his arm and stop the flow of blood.

There wasn't a stem of grass left within a mile. He unslung his cudgel and chewed through one end of the packing-tape strap. He tied the free end around his arm above the wound and pulled it tight with his teeth. After a while, the bleeding stopped.

He had never been so thirsty.

Gerry knew that if he could find water soon, there was a chance he might recover. But without the protection of the troop, injured and unable to use his cudgel, he had no defense against the predators that would soon be coming for him.

His one hope was to get to his parents' camp.

He had a rough idea of the direction it lay in. He might miss it, but he couldn't miss the river. And once he found the river he could follow it to the camp.

He started walking. The blackened earth crunched beneath his feet, and they were soon covered in soot. The ash stuck to everything it touched, including the blood covering his arm.

Now and again Gerry paused to loosen the tourniquet. He knew that he couldn't leave it tight all the time or his limb, starved of blood, would die. But if he loosened it too often, he would just as surely bleed to death.

Gerry was horrified at the extent of the fire. Maybe he had saved the troop, but how many other animals had died in the flames? So far he had passed several charred remains of what he guessed were mice, but he saw no other animals.

He was so thirsty.

He trudged on through the dark and silent landscape. Not a cricket chirped nor a bird peeped in that blackness. The only sound was the steady crunching of his own footsteps.

After half an hour, he paused to listen.

A warm wind ruffled his fur, and Gerry heard the faint tinkling of ash rolling over the ground. A last few embers glowed and ticked in the dark, and then the silence was complete again.

Good, thought Gerry, and for a minute he just stood there, swaying in the dark. As soon as he felt his eyelids growing heavy he roused himself. He had a feeling that if he fell asleep again, he would never wake up.

He urged himself on and thought about the troop. They had probably been able to outrun the fire, but by now they were likely just as tired and confused as he was. Gerry wondered if they would cross the burnt ground to return to the sleeping rocks immediately, or move on to some other place until the grass grew up again.

He realized, then, that he was worried about them. He had come to think of himself as leading the troop and now there was no one to make decisions for its benefit. He knew that this was a ridiculous and arrogant notion. Baboons did not require leaders and had survived without them for millions of years. The thought that they somehow needed Gerry was laughable.

As he trudged on, trees loomed against the stars. A few had survived the fire and appeared almost untouched. Others were like burnt matches. Then he felt grass underneath his feet again. For some reason, probably the wind, it had never reached this area. At about the same time, he thought he could see a dark line of trees poking above the horizon. He was nearing the river.

It seemed to take a lifetime to cover that final mile, but at last he found himself walking through a narrow gallery forest of acacias, and the scent of water reached him through the trees.

He staggered down the bank to the water's edge without even stopping to listen. The chorus of frogs and crickets fell silent as he crashed through the underbrush. Anything could have been waiting for him, but he was too thirsty to care. Gerry crouched at the water's edge and drank his fill. His thirst satisfied, he became aware again of the pain in his arm. He was unable to move it at all now, and while the arm throbbed his hand felt dead and numb.

He sat up again and strained to hear some sound. At first, there was only silence. The weird trilling of a clawed frog calling from beneath the water drifted into the air, and one by one the other frogs joined in, peeping and rasping.

Gerry didn't recognize this reach of the river, but he was certain that the camp was somewhere upstream. He started along the narrow flood plain, moving against the current. Traveling in the shallow gulch confining the river was a risk because it was almost impossible to hear anything down here. The singing frogs and whispering water drowned most of the sounds that would alert him to predators. But if he kept close to the riverbank, sooner or later he would cross the trail leading down from his parents' camp to the rocks where they drew their water. Traveling through the grass would have been safer, but if his father had already gone to bed, Gerry might easily pass their tents in the dark. This was the surer way of finding them.

He walked for what seemed a long time, pausing now and then to listen. He began to wonder if he had somehow missed the trail, and twice he nearly turned back. But then he felt the ground grow harder beneath his feet and he found himself on the path. He followed it up the bank and onto the veldt.

Clearing the trees, he saw a smudge of light in the darkness ahead of him. He began walking faster, and he soon recognized the lantern glow from inside their sleeping tent.

As he rounded the tent, he saw his father sitting before a small fire, slumped in a folding chair and reading by the light of tiny lamp clamped to the edge of his book. It was a gift that he had given his father a few Christmases ago. Ian looked up and saw Gerry standing at the edge of the flickering orange light. He peered at him over the tops of his reading glasses.

Gerry didn't know what to do, but he knew that he didn't have much time in which to do it. He approached his father slowly, casting his eyes downward. When he got very close, his father stood up, wary.

"Joan…" he said, never taking his eyes off Gerry.

Gerry could tell his father was nervous. Years in the field had given him a deep respect for the tempers and boundaries of wild animals. He tried to think of some way he might reassure his father. All he could think to do was to present to him.

Joan came out of the tent just as Gerry's father held out his hands, palms upward. This was standard practice for his parents when faced with a baboon who was begging. It was to show the animal that he had no food.

Gerry reached out and took his father's open hand.

Joan's mother brought a hand to her face and said something, but he couldn't make out the words. He thought maybe he heard the word "God." It was as if she were speaking a foreign language. She pointed to Gerry's injured arm, and Ian pulled her hand away, fearful. Then both were speaking gibberish punctuated with a few words he recognized: Joan. Ian. Kondoa. It seemed that the only words that still had any meaning for Gerry were names.

Soon they were arguing over something. Or was it just a discussion? People speaking a foreign language always sounded as if they were arguing.

And then Gerry heard something that filled him with hope.

His mother said his name. At first he thought he was imagining it, but then he heard it again, clear amid the gibberish. And now they really were arguing. His mother seemed to be trying to convince his father of something.

All Gerry could do was nod every time he heard his name, which drew a look of astonishment from both of them. They stared, open mouthed, as Gerry looked directly at them and nodded again. He had a moment of doubt in which he struggled to remember whether nodding or shaking your head meant "yes." He was pretty sure that nodding his head meant yes, but he had grown very unsure of anything to do with human habits.

When they resumed arguing, Gerry began collecting pebbles from the ground around the campfire. He had formed the first letter, B, when his parents looked down and saw what he was doing.

He heard his father utter a sentence with the word "God" in it.

Every time Gerry lifted his head to look at his parents he felt his head spin and he had to hold still for a moment to keep from blacking out. He searched the ground for more pebbles, but he had almost cleaned out the area around the campfire.

Joan said something to his father, then got to her knees and began sifting through the grass, collecting more pebbles. She gathered a little pile of them and placed them at Gerry's feet. She repeated her order to Ian and, with a look of resignation, he also began searching the ground.

Gerry could concentrate on writing his message now. One tiny stone at a time, he formed the letters to spell BRING GERRY HERE.

At least, that was what he had meant to spell. But when his parents came back to him with their hands full of stones, they stared hard at the words for a long time, saying nothing to one another. Gerry looked up at their baffled faces, then back down to the words he had formed in the dirt. This time he saw only a jumble of letters. Some of them weren't even letters. It was just a random pattern of rocks.

His mother's expression reminded Gerry a little of the last time she'd seen his report card.

Then Ian retrieved a game of Scrabble from the tent and showed the box of letters to Gerry. But he did no better with the wooden tablets. The words he formed looked perfectly reasonable one moment and the next they were nonsense.

After a while, his mother came out of the tent with a sausage and an orange, which she peeled for Gerry. His parents argued more. Ian kept pointing at the sausage as Gerry ate it, while Joan indicated Gerry's injured arm.

After he had finished eating, she extended her hand and Gerry took it. She led him inside their sleeping tent and took a first-aid kit from underneath her cot. It was a latched metal box similar to the one he had found in the plane. She sat him down on the cot, then took out bandages and a needle and thread, and Gerry realized that she was going to stitch his wound. He also knew it was going to hurt.

Or maybe not. At the same time, his father removed another familiar case from underneath the cot. In it, Gerry recalled, was a tranquilizing gun that his parents had once used to dart baboons so they could take samples of their blood. Gerry tried to see past his mother, who put a hand under his chin and seemed to be trying to focus his attention on her.

Then she set down the threaded needle and began to groom Gerry—parting the hair on his neck and head and running her fingers over the skin. She spoke calmly to him. The words went by in a babbling stream, and occasionally he heard his own name. Soon, drowsiness overcame Gerry, and he felt his eyes closing. He remembered feeling the cot sag beneath him as his father sat down beside him, hiding something in his hand. *I see it*, thought Gerry. *I see what you're doing*, but he was too tired to move.

Just as his eyes were about to close completely, he found himself staring at the lid of the first aid kit. On it was a red cross on a white background.

Gerry thought of the hospital where his body was being kept. He got up and looked around the room and found a picture of him in their yard back home in Croydon and brought it to the first aid box. He pointed to himself in the picture, and placed it on top of the red cross on the white background. He left it there for a moment, hoping the idea would sink in. *Gerry in hospital.* Then he picked up the picture and put it down in the center of the tent's dirt floor. *Gerry here.* He did it again. And again. *Bring Gerry here*, he wanted to say.

His mother watched him for a while with a baffled expression and said something to her husband. But his father wasn't listening. He was standing directly behind him. Gerry felt a brief, stinging sensation in his shoulder, but it was gone again almost before he could react.

He was asleep almost before his mother could guide him back to the cot.

OUT OF HIS MIND

Before he even opened his eyes, he heard a sound like slow breathing—the throbbing hiss of a Coleman lantern in need of pumping. He looked around the tent, which was lit by a dim, pulsing light. Soon, the lantern would go out completely, but he knew that he couldn't pump it up again with only one hand.

He still lay on his mother's cot. He looked down and saw that his arm had been bandaged in a tidy splint. Its whiteness was marred by a blotch of red spreading through the gauze, but from the look of it the bleeding had nearly stopped.

He sat up, and his head seemed to swim around the room. He felt a little stronger, but the pain in his arm was, if anything, worse. He crawled to the end of the cot and poked his head outside the tent. It was still dark. His father sat in a folding chair before the remains of a fire that had burned down to a few glowing nuggets. There was a book on his lap and the camp rifle lay on the grass beside him. His head drooped forward, chin on his chest. Gerry couldn't see his face but guessed he was sleeping.

He lowered himself to the ground and went to the bowl of water his mother had left for him. He picked up the bowl with one hand and drank until it was gone. When he looked up again, his father stood in the doorway, the rifle slung over his shoulder and a flashlight in hand. Ian rubbed his eyes and said something to Gerry. He came into the tent and pumped up the lantern, but it was nearly out of fuel and began to dim again almost immediately. He looked at the lamp and said something. Then he picked up an empty bucket sitting just inside the door, pointed toward the river, and walked out of the tent.

Standing in the doorway, Gerry watched his father carry the bucket past the fire to the trailhead at the edge of the trees. A moment later there was a brief flash of light as the path turned and Ian headed down to the river. And then he was gone, swallowed by the night.

Gerry walked outside the tent and circled around behind it. The Land Rover was gone. Had his parents figured it out? He felt a thrill of hope: what if his mother had gone to Kondoa to retrieve his body?

The trip would take hours. How long had he been asleep? He glanced at his wrist, expecting to see a watch there. It seemed a lifetime since he had thought of measuring time in anything less than days.

It felt strangely comforting to be back in camp after all he had been through. Gerry found it reassuring to finally know his parents were doing something to help him—his father fetching water, and his mother driving from Kondoa, surrounded by the roar of the Land Rover's heater. Gerry looked down at the pure white of the bandage around his upper arm. It seemed almost phosphorescent in the darkness.

He was walking back toward the door of the tent when he heard a cough from the direction of the river. Only one animal coughed like that, and Gerry knew there was a leopard in those bushes. It had almost certainly been watching Gerry since he left the tent.

He took two steps toward the tent's door before turning directly to the canvas and trying to duck underneath it, but his father had staked down the walls. With only one working hand, Gerry couldn't lift it far enough to slip inside. Facing in the direction where he had heard the cough coming from, he backed around the tent and headed for the door.

Inside, it was nearly as dark as it had been outside. Only the mantle of the lantern glowed a faint red. Gerry could only hope that the leopard would not come into the tent, but with the smell of his blood on the air, it was indeed a faint hope. He pulled down the zipper, closing the mosquito netting. It wasn't much against a hungry leopard, but it might slow it down a little. He debated whether or not to try calling his father. It might trigger the cat's attack, and there was almost no chance Ian would hear him. In the end, he screamed as loudly as he could, but knew that his father wouldn't return in time. He was on his own.

Gerry began searching for anything he could use as a weapon. Between the two cots was an overturned cardboard box that his parents used as an end table. His father sometimes kept a pocket knife there but it was gone. Their other rifle was almost certainly in the Land Rover. The only other place it might be was in the metal lock box.

Gerry went to the box. On the latch was a combination lock. He was surprised that the numbers came to him: 4 - 22 - 29. But of course all of the symbols on the dial were unreadable.

Then he saw the wooden case for the tranquilizing rifle lying on his father's cot. Inside it was a bottle of the tranquilizer and a hypodermic needle used to fill the darts. Gerry tore the wrapping from the syringe and just stared at it and then the bottle.

He'd done this before. He knew that he had to get the liquid in the syringe. But now, when he looked at it, just how he might accomplish this miracle escaped him. He jabbed at the glass bottle with the needle and tried to think. He had to unwrap something. The cap. He fumbled at the foil covering the top of the bottle.

And then he heard the mosquito netting at the far end of the tent starting to tear. He stopped moving, just to make sure he had heard it.

There it was again. He tried not to panic, but couldn't help the faint bleating noise coming from his own throat. Filling the syringe with one hand seemed impossible. He had to push the trembling needle through the membrane in the bottle's cap and hold it there while trying to withdraw the plunger with his teeth.

Gerry heard the ripping sound again and his hand began to shake, which wasn't helping.

He withdrew the plunger as far as he dared without pulling it completely free. But even with the hypo filled and in his hand, he knew the drug would not act quickly enough. He had only one chance: rush the leopard and inject it while it was still caught in the door.

He turned in time to see the cat's head push through the torn meshing. Gerry charged, just as the leopard forced one of its paws through the hole. He brought the syringe down like a dagger on the cat's shoulder, at the same time depressing the plunger with his thumb. The leopard snarled·and snapped at him.

Gerry let go of the syringe and crawled underneath one of the cots.

The cat thrashed at the meshing with its other paw, trying to enlarge the hole, the syringe still bobbing at its shoulder. It was furious, and more determined than ever to get at him. It took it only a few seconds to tear the netting to shreds and then it was inside the tent.

Under the cot, Gerry was already trying to chew his way through the canvas wall of the tent but it was much stronger than the netting. He found one of the stakes with his teeth and pulled on it for all he was worth but it held fast.

And now the leopard had found him, and its paws raked his back with its razor claws. Gerry sprang to his feet, turning the cot on edge. He tried to pin the cat's neck to the floor using the frame of the bed, but with only one arm he couldn't hold it. The leopard slashed at the cot and pulled it aside.

The tranquilizer seemed to have no effect at all on the leopard. *It does not*, thought Gerry, *look the least bit tranquil.*

He backed away from the cat. With nothing between them and nowhere to hide, it was all he could think of to do to extend his life by the split second it would take the animal to leap the extra foot.

It wasn't fair. If only his father hadn't gone to the river, his mother might have returned with his human body. Instead, he was going to die as a baboon.

He screamed and the leopard sprang.

It was like being hit with a sandbag. The cat knocked Gerry to the ground and he felt its paws like a clamp on either side of his head. Gerry tried to cover the back of his neck with his one good arm and protect his throat with his chin but in an instant he felt the leopard's teeth enter the side of his neck, and then its hind claws raked down his belly and he felt a terrible spilling from deep inside him. Still, he struggled.

In the darkness he felt the leopard's smothering embrace, hot saliva, or was it his own blood, dribbling from the jaws crushing his neck. He smelled the cat's rank breath and then even that was gone because his windpipe pinched shut.

Gerry couldn't even draw a last breath. The darkness was complete.

Then he smelled a wonderful and familiar smell: his mother's hair.

A corner of the darkness lifted, and in it Gerry saw a plastic bag of some clear fluid hanging from the ceiling. On it were words, one larger than the rest: SALINE.

The whole room lurched and swayed, setting the bag swinging, and Gerry realized that he was moving. They were in an ambulance, moving over a dirt road. Then the rest of the darkness withdrew and he saw his mother's face, smiling at down at him.

He turned and saw that the bag was attached by a tube to a thin, pale arm. He raised the arm and spread his fingers. It was skinnier and whiter than he remembered it—but entirely human.

Then his mother hugged him again.

HOW I SPENT MY SUMMER VACATION

The doctors want me to write about it. They say I just dreamed the whole thing while I was in a coma—even if nobody's ever really had a coma like that before. They think writing about it will be good for me. Plus I think they just want something new to read. Most of that stuff they have in their waiting rooms is pretty old. Actually, they said that nobody has to read what I write if I don't want, not even Mom and Dad.

Mom and Dad want me to write it down so I don't forget it (like that's going to happen). Or so that even if I do forget, at least it will all be written down somewhere.

I think they believe me. Actually, I know Dad believes me because one night he admitted he was actually a bit jealous.

Mom said she didn't think that was really appropriate and then Dad looked all embarrassed but I'm kind of glad he said it just the same.

I worry about them sometimes—my parents. It was harder on them than me in some ways, thinking I was dead.

Not dead, really. My mom says she never lost hope that I would recover and that's about when Dad gets quiet because I think he thought I was gone for good, even if he would never say so.

It was especially hard for Dad right at the end. When he came back from the river and found me and the leopard both dead in our tent. Except that the leopard got up a little later and ran off. That nearly gave him a heart attack. But the baboon was really dead. And I suspect he knew that it was me. So what else could he think except that I was dead, too?

I think about that more than I want to. About being dead. Sometimes I wonder if that's what I was between the time I was a boy and the time I woke up as a baboon, while I was just lying there. When those ghost baboons or whatever they were came and leaned over me, I wonder what they were thinking. Mom thinks they saved me. That my body died in the crash, and that they found a place to put me until it healed again and was ready for my soul.

I think about that baboon a lot, the one whose body I went into. If Mom's right, then where did he go while I was him? And where is he now, now that his body is dead? Dr. Ngoliong says that the ghost troop was probably just him and some of his students on their rounds looking down at me, because a lot of students visited me while I was in the hospital. He says that a silver baboon is probably "one of the more flattering descriptions" he's heard from one of his patients.

Anyway, I guess I should stop talking about writing about what happened and just start writing about it. So here goes.

For almost eight months, I was a baboon.

Oh yeah. This is way better. I feel like a weight's been lifted. Those doctors, sometimes they seem dumb but I guess they really do know what they're talking about after all.

I want to go back to Tanzania and see the troop. Dad found them before we left. They made their way back to the sleeping rocks and he said that the new grass had already started to come up. He said that Hector and Sphinx were gone, though. He thinks they probably joined another troop. I hope so.

But every time I bring up going back, my parents change the subject. They say that it's probably best for me to be in school for a couple of years first. Of course, now that we're back in Croydon, I want to go back to Africa and my parents want to stay here. So guess what we're doing? Actually, I don't think that it's really that they don't want to go back.

I think they're afraid that if I get too close to the troop, it might happen again.

School's okay. Sometimes I wonder whether I should tell Milton what happened—I mean, he knows about the crash and that I was in the hospital for a long time, but he doesn't know about the rest. God knows he'd have a field day with it. That's if he even believed me.

As it is, he said to me, "You know what you should do, Gerry?"

I told him no, I didn't know what I should do. But I didn't really think he did either.

Dr. Nader asked me if I was going to tell other people, like the kids at my school, about the dream I had. I said I didn't think I'd be bringing it up at my next turn at show-and-tell, if that's what he meant. I get enough ribbing just for being home-schooled in Africa. Maybe I'll tell Milton someday, but for now I'm just going to keep quiet. That seemed to work pretty well for those months when I was with the troop. When you're a baboon, you don't want to seem too different from everyone else. It's just not a good idea. Sometimes I'm not even sure how good an idea it is when you're a person.

But I know one thing: living with the troop is hard. Living without it is impossible. Somehow, you have to find a way to fit in.

ABOUT THE AUTHOR

DAVID JONES GRADUATED from the University of British Columbia with a degree in zoology, though he also took creative writing courses. He combines the two subjects by writing about science and nature.

Since then, he has written radio plays, books on animal subjects from ducks to whales, scripts for museum exhibits around the world, and even an interactive show at NASA's Space Center in Houston. His other children's book is *Mighty Robots: Mechanical Marvels That Fascinate and Frighten*. He lives in Vancouver.